# THE AWAKENING

## What Lies Inside

# DAVINA REDDIC

# AUTHOR'S NOTE

I can't express in words how truly grateful I am that you are here devoting your time to reading my work. With that said, I'd like you to be aware of some sensitive content that may cause triggers for some people. In this story there is mention of graphic sexual intercourse, stalking, murder, rape and the treatment/lack thereof and diagnosis of mental health disorders. If any of this subject matter is offensive to you, please reconsider reading Em's story. The last thing I would want is to trigger or offend any of my readers.

I take triggers very seriously and anything written in this fictitious story that makes light of certain subject matter or is not realistic is done so in the interest of entertainment that best suits the fictional needs of the characters in this story.

Sincerely,

V.

# DEDICATION

To my husband, thank you for your unwavering support. For believing in me so much that I had no choice but to do it. Forever grateful for you. I love you.

To my babies I hope you find something in life that makes you as happy as you all make me. I hope you produce something in life that requires great creativity. I hope I make you as proud as you make me.

# ACKNOWLEDGMENTS

Ramona: Thank you for the feeling you had about me & for editing my first baby with such attention and staying true to my voice.

BETA Readers: Your feedback was pivotal and I couldn't have done it without you (JM, JC, CF, CC, DG, MS)

Jen H | Mel G | Cas W | Leah B | Alex G | Chris F | Nessa W | Toya W | Elaina M | Liya P | Halle O

My parents, siblings, extended family and friends your overwhelming support has not gone unnoticed.

Reader: Thank you.

# TABLE OF CONTENTS



**PT. 1: THE SHADOWS**

# PT. 1

# THE SHADOWS

# PROLOGUE

I watch closely as his towering figure strides across the room, exuding sex appeal in a subdued manner, though that's the only genuinely subtle aspect about him. His demeanor is reminiscent of a bull in a china shop, quite the contradiction but it works for him, *and me.* I'm not bothered by the way he projects his voice and pounds his fists to make a point like the others who are visibly uneasy in the otherwise quiet room. There's just something about him that's drawing me in, an unexplainable magnet pulling me toward him; we can call it fate if you'd like but either way, I can't seem to take my eyes off of him and honestly, I don't want to.

I study him intently and take mental notes. It's what I do. The way one tendril always rolls back to the front when he's pushing his hair out of his face. Or how his nostrils flare when someone says something he isn't in the mood to hear. I note the little things that only I would notice, like how his steps are so firm and present, like he's carrying a purpose and his toned muscles move so naturally, radiating an energy that is so effortlessly charismatic.

His stance is poised yet when he stands upright his posture shows some struggle or restraint as if he's spent a great deal of time bending unwillingly. He sweeps his fiery red curls away from his face and opens his mouth to speak. I notice the small chip on his tooth and I wonder about all the mischief he's gotten into or how many other scars with stories his beautiful body entails.

When he speaks, everyone draws in towards him like a compass needle placed in front of a magnet. I don't know if it's because they actually want to, or if they're simply afraid not to. His words are drenched in a wild passion that creates a frenzy among the group. Apart from the other attendees, spanned throughout the room are men in gray uniforms, carrying holsters donning badges with their ears perked up. His words start to stir the air for the storm that is to come. The security team if you can call them that seems to be on alert.

I think to myself, *"Mmm Hmm! He must be our keynote speaker of the day,"* I say with snark and a sly grin amusing only myself, but I can't say for sure. After all, I've only just arrived and there could've been someone who brought the house down right before him, and I am not one to guess. Guessing means you are unsure, and I am not comfortable with uncertainty.

I slide into an empty seat. Everyone else knows their place as they sit snugly in their spots as if they live here or there's some sort of assigned seating; but not him, he refuses to sit. He refuses in such a manner that the rumble of his voice captivates me intensely. With every labored breath he takes, he captures more of my attention.

His eyes are bewildered searching for something to latch on to when he meets mine, I welcome his fury and my eyes sink deeper into his green ones, and all I can think of is how gray it would be if he weren't here. I look around taking it all in, the sheer emptiness that would consume this place. If it weren't for him, this room would be a cold, lifeless, pit of mediocrity. He's genuine in his approach. The others are either faking it or really just don't deserve to be here in my opinion, but no one died and made me chief so my opinion doesn't matter, not right now. I don't need it to. They'll know when I do. Another pound of his fist to the table breaks the chain of my thoughts. I shake my head discreetly covering my mouth with my hand disguising the smile beneath. This man is setting my mind on a tailspin, and all I feel is fire rushing through me, warmth gathering in the pits of my stomach, and moisture gathering between my legs. I am trying to hold back my growing smile as I watch him. I realize it would be inappropriate to share the sentiment with the group as no one else appears to be as affected as I am. If I am being honest, I am turned on by his display and I realize that is also inappropriate given the circumstance. A pang of jealousy stabs me as I'm certain I'm not the only one he's caused to feel this way. I scan the room with tight breaths eyeing my competition. People wear masks all the time, hiding behind the facade of normalcy when what lies inside is boiling at the surface to escape. But I can see through them and the competition here is non-existent.

*Nothing to worry about here, babe. Nothing at all.*

I scan the other gentlemen in the room and can't imagine another man evoking the kind of response in me that he has. Dare I say it, love at first sight? Perhaps it is. I don't have any other logical explanation for my feelings. Maybe it's the familiarity, I can see myself in him, who I am now, who I was always destined to be. While in the other men here I can only see who I was, someone I never intend to be again. It was the very first gaze when my eyes met his and what we shared during it, our emotions were able to speak in a language beyond articulation. In those initial seconds when we formed our bond, the world became a backdrop, and the boundaries of reason dissipated. In those moments he was the center of my gravity. I have never felt that way before for a man. That's how I knew it was love and not just admiration. He was sent here for a reason. He was sent to me, custom-made to shake me out of despair and awaken me. I'm unsure who held me in such high regard to send him, but whoever orchestrated this divine intervention deserves my immense gratitude. Alas, this is where we met, not at all the meet cute described in movies, you know the kind, on a bustling decorated December Street or a cute café. We met here in the heart of despair. The walls here resemble blankets of snow in December, and the room I am in stretches out wide. Two glass windows sit on each side and allow just enough sunlight to peek through. There are dimly lit corridors with frames of abstract paintings hung a bit off center, that if you look at them long enough begin to merge into one another. I can almost taste the hauntingly beautiful air, but I'd rather be tasting him. I let my mind wander creating a flavor that suits him, I imagine him to be spicy with a hint of sweet that's layered in as a surprise. I can't concentrate on anything but him now and I am thankful for the distraction.

It's hard to be here happily under the pretense knowing your voice doesn't really matter and the higher ups rule the world. Everything in here belongs to them, the conference room we met in belongs to them, but the atmosphere belongs to us, if it weren't for the people in this room this place wouldn't exist. This place is full of those of us who belong together, the ones who think outside the box, those who are desperate to blend in—merely waiting to stand out. In here we belong because THEY say we do and I am not comfortable with that.

This isn't the first time I've been to a facility like this. I've been the spokesperson twice or thrice, so I know what it's like to run the show. I've witnessed others put on their best performances, but nothing like him. He is the one, I am certain from the moment our eyes locked… It was poetic and I am fond of poetry. You can't describe something like love or passion without being just a bit poetic.

*This, oh this…this is magic instilled in madness, a brewing obsession, one glance and he's captured me, in a way I've never been before. For what is an obsession if its root awakening is not in love.*

# CHAPTER 1

# SHADOWS OF AWAKENING

"Ughh!" I groaned at the onset of consciousness. I didn't want to start my day yet; it was too cold and entirely too dark. My skin was glowing with goosebumps as if I needed any proof other than the sight of my breath swirling in front of me. I wiped away the cold sweat but chose to stay put, wanting to sink deeper into the mattress, despite the nagging urge to come to. It was winter here in Atlanta, which can get cold but not snow cold. So the frigidness in the air didn't add up. *No. No. on the other hand that wasn't true.* It was fall. I knew this because there was a little girl next door who had just celebrated her September birthday. She'd turned four, and on the day of her party it seemed like the last hint of summer rolled away. I had been opening my windows letting the crisp air rush in when I noticed her. Her party hadn't started yet, but she was outside oozing with anticipation of her guests' arrival. I looked out the window towards her and smiled, she was bursting balloons with her tiny feet. Wearing a purple-pink polka dot dress with her mid-length hair swaying along with her. She spun in endless circles as leaves danced from the trees before the camera her dad held, and I wondered if she felt as dizzy that day as I did now. Lying here, my head stuck on spin cycle, I cursed myself for that extra glass of wine last night. One, because I didn't finish it and not finishing it was clearly alcohol abuse and two, because I didn't need it.

My brain lingered a little longer on that day, I should have climbed out of the bed, pulled myself together and gone outside. There was nothing stopping me but me. We were invited, and I wanted to go, but I was wallowing in self-pity. I kept telling myself, what difference would our presence make? We didn't have kids to bring along, we would just awkwardly mingle with other parents, completely not being able to relate to them at all. I settled for sparing myself the embarrassment and for bringing her a gift later. I looked at it all anyway from the comfort of my room, punishing myself further.

I did this often lately, this self-inflicted punishment of staring out the window and wishing it was me in the house next door. We lived on a cul-de-sac, and beside us was a small family of four. The little girl next door was painfully cute. She'd always catch us coming and going and give a big hug, or tell me how much she loved my hair, or that my lips looked pretty. She was so polite for her age and so smart; her parents naturally adored her and they would go all out for their little one's birthday bashes – with a backyard zoo, a cotton candy maestro, and a DJ cranking up the tunes. No surprise there, they had enough energy, money, and time to go all out.

Don't get me wrong, it was adorable and all, but sometimes it was… an unnecessary display of wealth, or I always suspected it was the mom's way of making up for other shortcomings like her lack of being truly present. Of course there's a story there, there always is.

I mean a petting zoo in the city? A thirty-foot python at a kid's party? A cotton candy artist? Children didn't even care about a fluffy, dog-shaped sugar cloud. They would eat it if it looked like a pile of shit as long as there was sugar involved.

I couldn't help but roll my eyes; maybe I was just not so secretly annoyed. What were they thinking when they called in the DJ? To remix Ba Ba Black Sheep and Twinkle Twinkle Little Star for their four-year-old? Was a speaker not enough?

I suck my teeth, partially annoyed with myself because I think there's a jealous woman inside of me who I try to ignore but who loves to talk shit. I bet, if I were in their place, I would in a heartbeat do the same. Sitting alone and observing it all wasn't helping me much, but I couldn't help myself. I had a semi-excusable reason for being a bitch; my longing for children of my own made me a nasty witch sometimes, I couldn't help my envy. At times it just consumed me.

If I turned away from my jealous tunnel vision, for just a second I'd say that overall, I thought the family was great. The mom did everything with grace, she was kind, insightful and mainly she had been a great friend to me. A really great friend actually she was always intune with me; she knew when I was a bit off and made checking in on me her business, which should be the least of her worries but she still did it. The family wouldn't be complete without the little girl's older brother who was equally adorable. He was only six, but he was really good at baseball. I mean I'd catch him tossing the ball in awe sometimes of his speed and accuracy. I'd been over there a few times and overheard him reading children's chapter books at 6! I was impressed. Leigh was really out doing herself in the mom department and her husband never complained to Jay because if he had I would've known so she must be pulling her weight in the wife department, too.

So, apart from my neighbor Leigh's beautiful kids, it was safe to assume her marriage was pretty solid. I mean, come on! Her husband was a gem. He helped her around the house, was her personal masseuse, I always witnessed him opening and holding doors for her, pulling out her chair like a gentleman. She would gush over the fact that he remembered the details of what she liked and didn't, and supported her financially and emotionally as well. He was probably every woman's dream, an undercover Prince Charming or something. I gathered all of this intel from the multiple wine nights my neighbor and I used to share, a lot more often than we do now.

*Don't you miss that normalcy?*

Leigh was my friend, but I use the term with caution now. My success rate with friends isn't very high and my last friendship didn't last. I knew Leigh well enough though that she earned the title, but we grew distant which was wearing heavy on my heart and mind. We barely had time to see each other, mainly because I was dealing with some conflict and Leigh had been preoccupied with her kids and I knew her husband, much like Jay, traveled a lot for work. Leigh was also a bit of an introvert; she only really came out if it was something of grave importance to her or if I needed her.

*Sometimes, inside is the safest place to be.*

I didn't want to distance myself from Leigh. She brought out a side of me that I missed, but some things you just can't control.

Shit. I realize I sound like I don't like them, or like I am some judgmental nosey neighbor, but that isn't the case I truly do like them. I missed her, my neighbor, friend and her kids more than I could comprehend. I missed her kids and the special bond I had with them. I practically watched their family grow. We moved in right around the same time she was pregnant with her son.

I had to make a note to myself: *Clear an evening in Jay's schedule. Invite them over for wine. Serve them dinner. Buy whiskey for the guys. Lay board games out for the kids.*

Seriously, my gosh. It was really cold in my room. The chill in the air was so crisp that it was tough to convince myself, for sure, that it wasn't winter as I had initially suspected. I had turned the heater on the night before to 74 degrees, which was my ideal. Not too hot but not too cold. Enough to throw one leg out of the comforter and still be okay, but now I was shivering. The digital screen reads 64 from what I can see while still laying here… or was it called a monitor? Either way it read 64 so, I didn't know what happened. I must have forgotten, or I was too drunk to manage to turn it on correctly.

If I had placed a thermometer under my tongue, then I'm sure the mercury would have probably declared me a corpse. Without looking at my fingers, I knew they were turning blue and purple, resembling plums exposed to the frosty air all night. I should have rubbed my hands together and brought them back to life, that's what a normal person would do, not me; Instead, I closed my eyes for a few moments more and let the cold devour me.

If it was this chilly inside, it was safe to say that there was no way in hell I would be willing to step an inch outside of this space today, but I would have to eventually get out of the bed at the very least.

I could see that there were lights on throughout my home, but they were dim and I couldn't seem to grasp the memory of turning them on nonetheless a dimmer. If I was turning lights off, they'd be off. I preferred being in the dark these days anyway so after a few glasses I could pass out in peace! Darkness was peaceful, nothing to deal with if you couldn't see or hear it.

At this moment I actually couldn't tell you if it was daytime or if the night had snuck up on me. "Jay?" I called out but to no avail. "Jay?" I questioned loudly as my eyebrows furrowed. I was always met with silence whenever I spoke. As if I hadn't actually spoken at all."Oh. Right." I slapped myself a little harder in the head than I meant to.But I don't know why I was yelling for him when I knew that Jay wasn't here.

*He wouldn't be here. He couldn't.*

I knew that he was gone for a business trip for 2 days and still it seems… I completely forgot.

*That's not unlike you.*

Jayson was accustomed to traveling. Not that it was a passion of his, but he did it with ease. He packed meticulously, his itineraries were planned to perfection, and his hotels had every accommodation. He was a baseball scout, so going to visit places and living out of a suitcase had become his way of life. He was lucky enough to reach heights in his career and I never had to worry about our monthly expenses. We always had a fridge and pantry full, good clothes to wear, and no financial burden on our shoulders. I could comfortably be home while he worked. Comfortability was important to me. I had the freedom to freelance though I didn't have the balls to just quit altogether like I should have because whatever he earned would always be more than enough for the two of us. So my devotion to my boss wasn't out of financial constraints. Though sometimes when he was home it felt like we had the expense of a full-blown family. I wouldn't consider us wealthy, though, but I do believe that we belonged to the upper middle class. We weren't millionaires who could buy a premium designer bag every day, but if I needed a new one for an event, I could do so without any hesitation. Our bank account also paid for my monthly wine subscription, but with the way I felt this morning, I wanted to cancel it.

I felt like a semi-truck had hit me head on, and two walls were squeezing my temples with full force. From the moment I opened my eyes, I couldn't make sense of what was around me due to the intensity of the pain. I woke up feeling thirsty, lightheaded, and as if the world was ready to collapse onto my skull. The right side of my head was throbbing from the front to the back, and even the dimmest of lights seemed to pierce my vision.

"Yeah, that's it, I'm canceling this damn subscription! I mean it!" I winced, holding my head in my hands.

*"Oh please, you're not going to cancel it. It's already too late*

*for you."* A voice whispered mockingly.

I looked around, but there was no one in the room except me. It almost seemed like my heart had made its way up to my head and was beating rapidly, increasing my anguish. The only conclusion to what caused my migraine to erupt was the 8 glasses of wine I had the night before. But who's counting?

"Seriously! Get yourself together." I muttered as I lazily dragged myself out of bed.

For all intents and purposes I believe I stood up, and in front of me was my vanity mirror. My reflection was haunting, staring right back at me. I was unrecognizable, my eyes were sunken yet swollen, and I looked very pale. I leaned towards the mirror and pulled my lower lash line downwards.

"Great. Severely dehydrated." I sighed; I was a mess.

*You weren't even this bad before you stepped it up.*

My limbs felt heavier than usual. I didn't like this feeling. I had worked very hard for the body I have now and she would be very disappointed to see me in such bad shape. I had to force myself to go down the stairs, slowly taking each step. Mentally preparing myself for each and every movement. I've concluded that the only fix to my hangover readily available to me was 32oz of water, a big chug of coffee, and two eggs with toast from what I recalled was in my fridge at the moment. I wondered how I would muster up the energy to make myself some breakfast. Every sip of water I drank seemed to have absorbed into my body; somehow, never quenching my thirst like those poor hospital patients who just get ice chips and sponged water to their lips. Or moms in labor who can't drink until they expel a damn baby.

Honestly, this mundane routine was wearing on me. I began to question if I was being entirely honest with myself. I felt dissatisfied. Being a stay-at-home wife wasn't fulfilling. I guess if there's enough freedom, it eventually corrupts the insides. I have proven that to be true.

I wasn't obliged to do anything. I wasn't forbidden from much either except the obvious.

*HA!*

I would stroll around the rooms and sink into the sofa whenever I wished. Afternoon siestas were no stranger to me. The ceilings of our house kept me company for most of the day, and I stared at the blank white walls that Jay insisted on, all night. The only room that brought energy was my study, complete with a velvet green couch and blood red walls. Even if I completed all the house chores, I cooked, cleaned, and did the dishes, I still had plenty of time to do nothing. That's why I worked when the emptiness consumed me.

I was good at what I did. I'd have no problem reaching targets and converting marketing strategies to concrete sales; I would jump in to do that hybrid for my previous company as my ex-boss and I needed to distance ourselves from time to time, she can be well overbearing. I still felt a void though.

Our house was always empty, and I blamed the emptiness on not having kids of my own. I wanted to be a mother, but my innermost thoughts made me doubt my capabilities. Nonetheless, I was willing to try. I kept trying.

I opened the fridge and reached for a semi-ripe avocado, spreading it neatly onto my toast. When my taste buds regurgitated the merlot from last night, it was at that time I decided to make myself another mental note.

*Tree-toppers vineyard. Merlot is the fucking devil, don't drink that shit again. You hear me?*

I watched my figure in the reflection of our television screen and touched my womb. I gave myself a cringe worthy pep talk, "Better change your mental, better eat up, manifest all the things you desire," and, "try that damn placenta tea that won't be the thing to kill you," and, "while you're at it leave the merlot alone."

*It's not what you really like anyway.*

"Turn from me to we." I hummed with a sad smile plastered on my face, imagining the day I would have a baby growing inside of me. Again.

*Not in the cards for you was my initial intruding thought.*

One of the fertility awareness groups I was in suggested the dried-up womb of another woman to sip on to increase my chances of getting pregnant. But after the initial absolutely not wore off I thought, "Yeah, well. I was crazy anyway, so it didn't matter much to me. I'll just try it."

I had some placenta tea leaves in the cabinet so I opened the packet and almost puked at the pungent smell but pressed on.

*Anything is better than that merlot, man up, don't be a little baby.*

*Slurp, slurp, drink, drink. Take it to the head.*

I had put on a mindless reality show for background noise while I boiled some hot water. I sat down with my tea to binge-watch, while I repeated mantras about fertility over and over. Another crunchy suggestion from the group was to "manifest."

Jayson and I had tried everything, and I would always be disappointed by failure. It was weird; we would be nearly sure that the pregnancies were viable. I'd even gain weight each time I got a positive test. I'd gone through all the appointments until the day my womb was just empty once again. Oddly enough Jayson never made mention of our efforts falling in vain. He did that to protect me, I'm sure. He'd be a great father. I see him with the neighbor's kids and he treats them as if they were his own. Probably the stem of my jealous thoughts. I've always been pretty territorial and I don't care if they are just children.

It was still pretty dark outside, so I checked my phone.

*9 A.M.? What? This makes no sense.*

*When did Atlanta become Alaska?*

I pulled the notification bar down, and to my surprise Jay had not even bothered to check up on me.

*No, I miss you—zero care about my whereabouts, whatsoever.*

*Where would you go?*

I don't really care that he hadn't checked on me. It's the fact that because of that I now had no idea what he was up to. That bothered me a little more than I'd like to admit. However, my tender-hearted mother left me a billion voicemails, "Where have you been, my dear?" Her voice was filled with affection. "Please respond, okay? Honey Bee?" Ironically, my mom was lonely like her daughter. Who else would text me if not her? She never married my father, and they broke up when I was three. So, I guess that pretty much meant all she had was me, and him in between his flings that never lasted long. I think he loves her; she just wasn't enough. Enough of herself for anyone not even her and surely not me. She just was.

I felt my neck stiffening, so I readjusted my posture and plopped onto the sofa. I scrolled some more mindlessly and paused when I saw "Daddy." My dad had left me a few messages as well. "I miss you," and, "I love you no matter what tomorrow brings."His messages are simple and to the point. I quickly replied to my mother, clicked the phone shut, and threw it towards the other sofa. "Goddamn it! This hangover might just take me out!" I dug my fingertips into my temples and squeezed my eyes shut. I wasn't in the mood for chit-chat with my mom, or bragging on Jay to my father. I couldn't allow myself to stir on why I haven't heard from my husband, I just needed rest.

# CHAPTER 2

# THE BONES

I walked the 20 blocks from my place to the baseball stadium where I met Jay officially. Not what I would typically choose to do in my spare time but, honestly, I only went there to eye the hot guys on the diamond and chug a few good pours of wine from the all-inclusive bar inside of the luxury box my boss secured till I couldn't think straight. I would not have attended a baseball game by myself or by my own accord; I could care less about baseball, after all. But alas my boss invited me under the guise of a celebration for my success aka an offer I couldn't refuse. Because it wasn't really about me at all. There was a reason she picked a baseball game; I'll only be made privy to the truth when I get there or after whatever she needs done is done.

*Ah. Her. My Boss.*

*Barbara.*

When Barbara said jump you said how high, when Barbara was heading your way you moved, when she invited you to something, I cannot think of anything stupider to do than to say no, so I went. I am calculated, to say the least. Barbara doesn't intimidate me; if anything, I see her as someone to learn from, and I need to keep her close to do just that. I had recently been promoted to becoming the director of sales at our workplace, Ingenuity Recovery—for my consistent hard work and ability to take her crap. Well, it wasn't a walk in the park to single-handedly manage the caseload of twenty people, along with hers when she was distracted. Which was often lately.

Rightfully, she wanted to give me a treat. Show her appreciation if you will for my record-breaking sales.

I would've much rather preferred a bonus, but Barbara is so far removed from her staff that she wouldn't know staff appreciation if it kicked her in the ass. She's more of the look down on you from her glass tower. Put donuts in the break room for the peasants and think she's a woman of the people.

Yeah, so, Barbara has different tastes. She's fond of a crystal cocktail glass filled with an aged whiskey, neat. Or Jameson if she isn't trying to impress. She keeps a copy of the Wall Street Journal on her desk and she wouldn't be caught dead in anything but a Little black dress. She thinks men are just disappointments waiting to happen and she can pleasure herself without one. She is woman, hear her roar. So on and so forth. But she's made a name for herself, a well-respected one and while the bonus would've been nice the trade-off of rubbing elbows and being on her good side wasn't so bad either.

At work, I sold a catalog of products and supplements to sports management firms and professional teams. The products were geared toward helping enhance the athlete's recovery post-workout, prevent injury, and increase endurance. I couldn't care less. I have no idea if they actually do what they say they do though the reviews are 90% positive. Initially I just wanted money to spend on my substantial wine collection, a nice place far away from my mother and the occasional bag or shoe; my desire to hold onto this job changed after a pivotal moment which required me to be in the exact position I am in.

It didn't take me long to figure out how to make myself an asset and that the best way to make sales was to sell what I had to offer.

I mean. Damn it! My looks were a godsend. I knew that the key to success was simple, red lips paired with a sleek ponytail, and a tightly fitted dress accentuating my curves. I learned from the best. I was gifted with angelic genes and a devilish smile; come on*! I had to use that to my advantage.* Plus, it worked for Barbara so borrowing a page from her book wasn't a bad idea and I'd read this book before it was a good one.

It helped my case that it wasn't unusual that most of my

meetings were with men. It is the world of sports. I would lure them in and sell my appeal neatly packaged in an Ingenuity Recovery contract, full of purchase order flows of pricey products. If they were foolish enough to believe I was truly seducing them then what a pity. I was doing it all for me and they were not my concern nor my problem once they signed on the dotted line. *I am whoever I need to be to make the pitch, to get what I want.*

The view at the game was nice. I could see the green baseball field stretching across from where we stood, hot men, running around and stretching... oof, now that I was here, I couldn't complain. *I wonder what the cost of season tickets is?* Barbara had booked us the luxury box seats that stood just above the field level. We had complete private access; which meant we could wine and dine without running the risk of overly excited fans spilling beer and peanuts on us.

The red plush sofa seats welcomed us, especially me. Red is my color of choice. I didn't know everyone in the box. I imagine Barbara invited whoever she felt needed to be there to create the best façade. Most of the people in the box wore business casual and by people I mean men. They looked as if they were plucked straight from their swanky office buildings, leaving half empty coffee mugs on their desks for their secretaries to tend to, hopped in their black town cars, loosened their ties and walked on in.

I was lost in thought entertaining myself stealing glances at the field when a man, wearing a midnight blue suit with pinstripes, caught my eye. My heart slipped straight through my chest into my shoes.

*Holy shit. It's him. His face, his smile.*

*Get a grip.*

*What were the odds of us crossing paths?*

*Cute.*

Jay was standing 3 feet away from us, and I couldn't register the fact that I missed noticing he was here earlier. "Who is he?" I pointed discreetly as I leaned in and whispered in Barbara's ear. I needed more concrete information. Really, I needed confirmation. "He is our company's next client… next target to be precise." She looked at him and smirked.

I wanted to throw her off the ledge of the box right then and there, simply for how her eyes twinkled when she looked at him, but I couldn't.

I shifted my focus and observed Jay. He was cool and collected and so charismatic, making notes and voice recordings after certain players showcased their stuff. He was personable, talked to the other gentleman in the box, had a firm grip when he shook hands and sipped the same amber liquid the entire time he was there. Drinking to be social but not too much because he was conducting business. Look at him, a display of excellent balance. I stored everything I had gathered in my mental notebook in a new Chapter called Jay.

He was six feet, four inches tall, with dark brown hair and mint green eyes. In the right lighting, his hair had hints of red, and his looks played with my heartstrings effortlessly. There was no doubt that Jay was a seriously handsome man with a killer smile, a stark contrast that stood between his porcelain skin and his darkly colored thick manicured beard. The silver cufflinks that illuminated his wrists were just enough to allude to status but not overly stated. Well done, Jay, well done. I liked that the way he presented himself reminded me of my father. A well-dressed business man was always a force to behold.

I would bet money that he could 100% charm his way into anyone's panties within 15 minutes. Tops. Ugh, I mean—I wanted to bury myself in his presence and my panties were practically at my ankles and he hadn't uttered a word to me. But he didn't need to. I knew I'd have him. I just needed to be patient, which I will admit wasn't my strong suit.

Barbara and I looked at him so keenly that he noticed us. Or he felt the hole our eyes were burning through the side of his face. He furrowed his eyebrows together as he looked at us from across the box and then his face relaxed into a wide smile. Jay looked as if he had recognized her, probably from our firm's advertisement.

I reassured the jealous voice in my head as he was advancing towards us.

Every step he took in our direction, my heart raced faster and faster.

*He's not on his way to declare love at first site, psycho, he doesn't know you. Yet.*

*Pull it together, you wouldn't want to lose him to her, would you?*

*Now is not the time to forget who you are.*

He came over and introduced himself. He seemed like a guy with zero childhood troubles, you know the kind that came from a loving two-parent home, the QB of his college football team, never worried about money but somehow, the way he spoke wasn't flashy or boastful. He was down to earth and funny and though he lacked a little fire he was everything I imagined he would be at face value.

That's why the fluttering in my chest and the moisture between my legs was all I needed to stay a safe distance away from him. I barely engaged in conversation with him other than the initial introduction and instead tried to watch the entire game. I couldn't mess this up.

I could have talked to him a lot more without throwing a wrench in my plan and I wanted to, but my cheeks were flushed, and my insides were tingling. The last thing I wanted was a one-night stand, so it was better to keep away, for now. Until I could put my plan into action. This was a divine encounter, sort of, and I had to proceed with caution.

At the beginning of the 8th inning, I felt a switch in my level of peace.

Jay was about to leave so he thanked Barbara, hugged her, and kissed her on the cheek. His lips lingered half a second too long because she had nudged in towards him, trying not to break the contact in between.

*My boss.*

*Ballsy witch.*

I couldn't stop my jaw from being clenched, and my eyes from narrowing. I felt a wave of bitterness directed straight towards Barbara. But I couldn't claim Jay; he wasn't mine to do so yet. What the hell was wrong with me? Why was I so jealous so fast? He's not *him*. That was different.

*He could have kissed your cheek, but he didn't.*

*He could have slung his arms around you and wrapped you in them.*

*You could have pushed Barbara aside and held her by her hair, yelling, "Back off!" but you didn't say a goddamn thing!*

I don't know why my body and mind reacted that way. Barbara

was an equally attractive woman, and she was single. She could do whatever she wished even if that meant Jay. She didn't know the plans I had for him and for that I couldn't blame her.

Given my level of confidence it was strange of me to be filled with envy that day.

*Pretty normal of you.*

I heard the mocking words as if they were blasted through a megaphone. I glanced to my left and right, but the only company I had was myself. *Shake it off, babe.*

I had just met him formally and any passing before this didn't count. It was ridiculous that I felt compelled to receive his affection so soon, he couldn't possibly understand he belonged to me. Thankfully, the jealous feeling didn't last, and I set off to do exactly what I would have done today if I hadn't been roped into attending the game.

I picked up my bag from the seat, mildly smiled at my boss, gently rubbed the plush red sofa because it made me smile inside and marched out of the box without looking back. All hail, my bruised ego.

*Who does she think she is? Dark haired siren.* I muttered under my breath as I made my exit.

When I finally got out of the crammed stadium into the street equally full of game attendees, I kept walking towards the East of the stadium at a fast pace. I was damn sure the whiskey bar I overheard the gentleman speaking of was up 4 blocks on the right and I was hell bent on finding it. I inhaled and exhaled some sense back into myself as I entered the bar. I knew I was being irrational and I like to check myself before I spiral. I smirked at the thought.

I reached the bar's entrance, found an empty stool, slipped my card out of my wallet, and counted in my head. My energy almost instantly felt different; I was feeling more like myself and counting the seconds before some man nowhere near my league would proposition me with a drink.

I slightly shifted in the stool and eyed the bartender. He gestured his head up at me and I mouthed, "Jameson, neat."

My beverage of choice was consistently wine since I've outgrown my vodka days; so why I was ordering whiskey was beyond me. I pressed my lips to the brim, hoping to calm down, but I was interrupted.

"Hey, sweetheart, what's your name? That drink's on me." A young man leaned towards me to catch my eye. He was good-looking, but he wasn't as handsome as Jay. Furthermore, that took 120 seconds. I was off my game tonight. I hated that.

He put his hand out to shake mine and pulled it up to his lips in what he thought was a suave move. I expended a lot of energy holding back my unimpressed face. I tried to listen to him, but my attention was diverted towards a woman who had passed me by, leaving a mist of her perfume lingering in the air. I could tell she was wearing Coco Bloom; I knew because the scent was one of my go-to's. I had seen her somewhere, but in my mind, her detailed image was blurry.

She still looked vaguely familiar from what I could make out of her which is why I was staring so intently at the back of her auburn-highlighted hair. Just waiting for the second she turned around. The man before me cleared his throat, and I broke off my trance.

"Yeah... uh, right, I am... Barbara." I said clearly uninterested, as I blinked my eyes.

Honestly, I was too distracted to listen to him. He was probably talking himself up anyways, and I was the least bit interested.

This is the part I dreaded most, the clean break where I need to leave and the homeboy feels like I owe him something because I let him buy my drink. I guess I needed to get this over with and end this lovely exchange, before Mr. 3 pc department store suit assumes I'm leaving with him. Poor guy, if I hadn't run into Jay he might've gotten lucky. I turned causing the stool back to swivel and crash into the handsome hand of Mr. Jay himself. I watched the amber liquid bead down his thumb. Reflexes or my vagina kicked in as I licked my lips and watched the bead until it was no more.

*Shit shit shit.*

"Well hello, B," he spoke calmly, smiling at me.

*How the hell long was he here?*

I'm assuming he heard me introduce myself to that dude.

Technically, I should have been embarrassed, but he played along and that stirred a bit of desire in me wondering how that role play would look. I can only assume the way I looked up at him, was a dead giveaway that I was going to be underneath him tonight. Department store suit didn't look too pleased. But c'est la vie.

I was a little awestruck as I gathered my belongings to leave with Jay. The truth was I couldn't believe how nicely this night had played out for me. There he was, finally in arm's reach and I just couldn't resist him. I just wanted to be in his arms, in his bed. It was taking everything inside me to stop myself from completely losing my mind. I wanted him badly, and I couldn't think of anything else. Well, except *him* sporadically.

Jay and I stayed for one more drink until he invited me back to his place for a night cap. To my surprise, Jay's place was opposite of what I imagined. I wasn't hoping to walk into a dull gray bedroom with just one framed photo of two boys and their parents. This was a wrench, but I could work around it.

He excused himself, and I plopped on his bed, kicking my heels off. I could hear Barbara reprimanding me for mixing business with pleasure. But I thought, she's just going to have to deal with this one. I was creepily… I will admit, smelling his pillows trying to take the scent of him in as deeply as I could, but I sat up when I heard Jay in the kitchen, opening a bottle with a pop.

He entered the room walking towards me barefoot with a confident smile, his shirt unbuttoned at the top revealing strands of curly dark brown chest hair. His hands cupped two champagne flutes filled with a golden liquid. I noticed the beads of prosecco resting on the back of his hand, and I restrained myself from licking them off. *I've got to get this licking fixation in check.*

Jay stared at me so intensely I could tell he was trying to read my thoughts. I must not be that deep because he knew damn well that my thirst was not going to be quenched with prosecco and it would only be satisfied by him. He needed no further cues; he took a sip from his glass and placed them both on the side table.

He gently turned to me and reached for my hands to stand me up. He turned me around gently leading me by my shoulders and grazing my neck with his teeth in a soft, tantalizing manner. He unzipped my dress and guided it down to my ankles. I spun to face him and he kissed me softly guiding me backward with a firm yet gentle pressure from his hips against my stomach, we moved in unison until I felt the mattress edge against the backs of my knees.

His hand caressed my face softly and sighs escaped my lips as he kissed me slowly and deep. He hovered on top of me and before he moved he opened his mouth, "Strip." he whispered, gripping the sides of my waist.

I felt a surge of urgency coursing through me, and my heartbeat raced. Jay must have noticed the change in my energy. He raised his eyebrows, questioning if I was okay with what we were about to do. I hesitated for a second, but quickly recovered, smiling at him.

I placed my hand on his bare chest and looked him in the eyes. I leaned in for a kiss, and just before our lips could meet, I pulled away, gently pushing him onto the bed.

*Such a tease. Bravo.*

I tilted my head towards him and calmly ordered,

"You will sit beneath me, watch, and never touch me. Your eyes will remain on me, and you won't be allowed to touch yourself. I will pleasure myself on the very edge of this bed, and you will not move. I will scream your name over and over again until I'm shaking. When I am done playing with myself, you will beg me, "Barbara, please," and only then will I allow you to devour me whole. You will thank me, and I will leave. Am I clear?"

*Well done, it was almost as good as the real thing!*

Jay's wild eyes became dilated, sparking a fire only I could see. The minty eyes he wore so well had hints of emerald and swirls of sage with flickers of amber and I couldn't believe what I saw. It was like a window, a direct channel to *him*. I was so caught up in that fire I wanted it to burn me. It made my climax that much more intense. I didn't even realize that Jay had obeyed my every word. I laid back panting completely satiated and beaming with pride, but remembered I needed to follow through, as to not disappoint her; so I got up and inched my panties back on followed by the rest of my clothing, kissed him on his cheek for good measure, and I left him there staring at me desperately wanting more. He had no idea I wanted more too, just not yet.

****

I obviously had access to Barbara's contacts so getting his number was child's play. I texted him coyly 2 days later asking if he was still in the spot where I left him. He liked that and he knew who I was immediately, so naturally we made plans for the following day. For our first actual date, I preferred to skip the fancy restaurants and instead chose to hang around at a local coffee shop. That day, our meetup was pretty casual, given the fact that he had a front row seat to my climax less than what, 72 hours ago?

There was no awkwardness between us, and we spent hours drinking coffee, eating perfectly golden-baked cookies, drowning ourselves in each other's lives. Nestled into each other in the shop's window seat bench. You'd think we'd been together for years the way the conversation just flowed and my body fit perfectly in the crevices of his.

I can thank the ambience for this ease. The coffee spot was cozy, dimly lit, and the warmth from the cup was rushing to my cheeks. I chose this place on direct opposition of Barbara's recommendation of a coffee shop in our new building as she told me she loved it, and don't get me wrong, the shop in our building makes a good brew and the photo opportunities are endless and genuinely I liked most things she recommended I don't know why I enjoyed everything she did something about the fact bothered me immensely. But since Jay was to be wholly mine, I couldn't risk tainting it with anyone else. Though this particular coffee shop held a special place in my heart.

Jay opened up to me about his struggles at work. He was good at his job, but he didn't feel fulfilled working there. His passion was to be a therapist.

It surprised me a bit, but it did make sense to me. He later told me that he lost his younger brother who had some struggles. His interest in mental health was sparked from his early years; growing up with his brother was tough and he studied psychology in college just to be an advocate for him.

*Bless it.*

He eventually completed med school and got into the first year of residency, determined to become a psychiatrist.

This man was academically driven. We didn't match in this aspect. I was driven but in other ways, I didn't have patience for school. I required instant gratification for everything I did in life. I could barely concentrate on my studies that final year with all the distraction, and I only worked hard just enough the night before an exam just so I could pass. Barely.

I went to a small private school, and Jay went D1. In the end, we both came out clean, but I would've been in heavy debt with student loans for a long while if not for my dad. Jay had a football scholarship to thank for his lack of student loans.

Everything was better than I could've imagined until our quaint table was filled with a third voice. To my disdain.

*Her.*

"B?" Jay questioned, as he kissed her hand hello while leaving me with the feeling he was kissing me goodbye.

*He called her my name.*

*That is not your name.*

I stared at him, my eyes conveying disbelief. My heart dropped to the ground again. His face showed confusion, but to ease the moment, I smiled.

# CHAPTER 3

# DISTORTED REFLECTIONS

"**F**uck!" I winced. If I was a weaker woman I would've been throwing up from the pain. Dreaming about Jay didn't help relieve any pain. I was missing him excruciatingly and all my idle alone time was in part to blame for the pain of this hangover.

The irony is that I'm living through hell on a Sunday. I'm certain Satan brewed this hangover himself, meticulously infusing it with venom. After taking pride in his work, he apparently had no one else to share it with but me. So, I'm the fortunate one he chose to grace with it, complete with a bow for formality's sake. I'd put money on the fact that I was hanging in the depths of hell by now. I was so cold. The damn heater wasn't helping me much, either. White square nuisance only increased my gas bill. *Seriously, why am I still freezing, I have to have Jay check to see if it's working alright.*

As I toss and turn and kick my legs like a toddler fighting with the bedsheets, I perk up and I can't believe this wasn't my first thought. I know exactly what I need. Greasy Chinese to wash my suffering down the drain. I was salivating at the thought, and only Chinese takeout could fix my current state, my mother taught me this.

*Mmm… deep fried spring rolls.*

*General Tso's chicken.*

*Sweet and sour pork.*

*I could polish off a pint of shrimp fried rice right now.*

I stretched my arms overhead as I sat up in bed.

"Ugh… where are you?" I groaned, sifting through the bed sheet and the blanket frantically.

"Ah ha! Found it." I grabbed my phone from underneath the green throw pillow and powered it on. I swear to God, I would do some strange things for some Chinese food right now. And obviously, due to my state of desperation the food delivery app was behaving painfully slow. I jammed my fingers into the phone, clicking at glazed short ribs with lightning speed.

To punish me further the screen suddenly blanked out as I was about to proceed with my order.

*Great.*

I stared at my phone for a second or two, willing it to turn back on with the order confirmation screen; a very long 25 seconds later, it at least came back on sans my order. Jay's name glitched onto the screen, and I quickly answered.

"Hello, Jay?"

"Babe… Hello?!"Nothing except silence followed.

*It's okay.*

*He must be stuck in an area with shitty signals.*

*The usual.*

I waited for a while and took a few breaths.

*Still, nothing?*

I dialed his number, attempting to call him back.

*Ringing… ringing… Ugh.*

The brightness from my phone was swallowing me, and I couldn't take it anymore. I ran my fingers through my knotted hair, took a deep breath, and threw my phone aside.

It wasn't anything outside the ordinary for him to be away, roaming around in seedy areas, but what was abnormal was this headache. I'd go to urgent care and demand a morph drip for the level of pain in my head right now. I would if I wasn't so turned off by the whole hospital thing.

*Of course.*

Jay will reach back out when he has better reception and another free minute. He's always got a full schedule when he's on the road. He searches high and low for talent both undiscovered and already established pros. He's at practices, dinners, games, farms, camps and so on and so forth. I traveled with him a few times exploring new cities playing tourists. We went to the big apple once, the vibrant streets of New York dazzled us, well me, they dazzled me. He had been there one too many times to still be impressed. Digital billboards gleamed, skyscrapers stood tall, and it seemed as if everyone was crowding into the streets because that was where they had to be. But with no real purpose at all. I could see why people were drawn to the city that never sleeps; for them, it was full of opportunities, full of places to hide, inspiration, you could blend in and stand out all in the same breath. Yeah, I could see the appeal.

*A part of me could always see the appeal in one thing or another.*

We had been casually dating for 2 months before this trip, the trip where we made it official. I flew in a day after him. The morning of my flight, I had hurriedly stuffed my carryon with four different lingerie, and a pair of sexy fishnet stockings. I managed to pack actual clothing as well and a makeup bag, but I for one didn't plan on having a use for them. I was looking forward to spending the weekend tangled in each other's limbs completely naked, his hands all over my body.

Barbara was out of town on business, so I had loose ends to tie up at Ingenuity which irked me the bigger we got the less I seemed to see of her at the office, and the more responsibility fell on me. It's not that I wasn't compensated richly because I was, it's just that I used to like being Barbara's right hand, I loved the energy she brought. This cocky confidence it was contagious, and she was fun, too. I admired her but things have changed. The confidence and comradery we once shared as this female duo was diminishing. I started feeling smaller in her presence, I started forgetting that I was a force even when we weren't tag teaming pitches. Not just at work, she was interfering in my personal relationships as well. She even inserts herself with my dad and the thought of that makes my soul itch. My dad was often popping into the office, and he would just light up when he saw her. They chatted for what seemed like an eternity about business, or the latest in the news, of course completely ignoring my presence. I didn't like it; I have a bit of a jealous side and I can be rather territorial. I didn't like how whenever she was present, she took over, maybe because that's something I am used to doing. I don't know and I don't care anymore... I can't pinpoint exactly when the flip switched on my feelings for Barbara, but I can't shake the feeling that she's getting off on trying to replace me where I matter most.

*One switch of a flip and I'm sure I could easily seize your role and take over.*

*I could be you so much better than you and no one would even remember you existed.*

I had to remind myself nothing was out of reach for someone as adaptable as I. I still couldn't help the intruding thoughts.

*A chameleon, who I need to be when I need to be...*

But before I could finish that thought my Jay opened the hotel suite door.

I surprised him with a little something special. We had both been so busy as of late and while facetime dates were cute and all, it was nothing like the real thing. I needed to do something so unforgettable that he'd be left in awe of me, that he'd crave me, love me. I wore a long tan trench coat that tied at the waist. Sheer black knee-high stockings and my favorite pair of nude red bottoms. I pin curled my shoulder length brown hair letting some fall sloppily about my collar bone. I saw my reflection in the window, the hotel lighting gives my hair an auburn hue in areas as if hair dye had faded in the perfect pattern. The perfect blend but unreliable as you don't know if it'll ever fade to perfection again or blend so seamlessly that one isn't overshadowing the other. I relished a bit staring at what I saw in the mirror. *Pretty,* I thought.

*Too bad it won't last.* I whispered to myself.

I was mostly satisfied with what I saw but made a mental note that it was time to get to the salon. Under my trench was absolutely nothing. I wore what I came into this world in. I changed in the lobby, this sort of thing always turned out well in the movies, so I was ready to try it.

*Remember who you are tonight.*

I closed my compact with a click and leaned into the bar. Confidence was my muse, but I didn't want to leave anything to chance and mess this up.

Just in case, I chugged a glass of merlot before I entered the elevator from the hotel's lobby bar, and to make sure I set the tone I put on a lip. Barbara had a signature red lip reserved for when she was standing on business. And since I was propositioning Jay to fuck me into next week tonight, I figured this constitutes business, so I borrowed another play out of her book. Jay opened the door, and I opened my coat. His eyes alone devoured me, but his mouth greeted me with a, "Well hello, B." It's become our thing. I used to be really tickled by it. It even turned me on to pretend to be her, but I need to come up with a new thing for us before this one gets too close. I've been B so much I sometimes forget I am me. Jay handed me the drink he had poured for me. Whiskey, neat. As he palmed my ass and pulled me in.

I could see that he was amused by my little stunt and fully erect at the sight of my body, but being the gentleman he was, he kept his composure until I was fully inside the suite.

I eyed him intensely as I bit my lip.

*This one was all mine, and I was all his.*

He was shirtless, in dress slacks, with no socks as his feet padded quickly toward the couch in the room I trailed closely behind. I went to open my mouth to protest. To take the lead as I had before. I liked to be in control. It's calming to me, but he put his finger up firmly, pressed it to my lips and shook his head no. *"Not this time,"* he said, I shuttered. Goosebumps shone on my fully exposed skin. He trailed his finger down from my lips slowly painfully, until he just grazed my clit. He didn't break eye contact and the intensity of his stare was making me sweat. He undid his slacks, let them fall to the floor and coolly sat on the couch. The floor to ceiling windows spilled light from the city scape red light danced on the wall and played in his hair illuminating the highlights. He looked up at me and for a fleeting second I saw *him* and it set my soul ablaze. The nerves I was feeling dissipated. It was an out of body experience. It felt so familiar yet different. It was how I imagined it would be yet not. I found comfort in the similarities. I don't know why I was falling for Jay. Was it because of Jay, or the fact that Jay was *him* just not fully?! The intensity of that fuck left me famished and dazed I couldn't think another thought if I tried so when Jay practically read my mind and asked if I was hungry, I leapt from the floor of the suite and squealed in excitement; we threw on comfy clothes and rushed into the busy NY streets and grabbed takeout from probably the best Chinese food spot I have ever had and trust me, I've had my fair share.

I am positive they failed the health inspection because damn!But I couldn't care less. When in Rome. It tasted like heaven coated in tangy, sweet sauces. My tastebuds were thanking the Chinese Gods, and to top it all off—it was hot and fresh and dirt cheap.

Back to our hotel, we hopped into the elevator. Jay's face was unreadable. I didn't like that sometimes he could just be so bland, so…

I didn't finish that thought because it wasn't fair to compare them so closely. I leaned into him to ask him what was wrong. Jay said nothing and that actually everything was right and he'd like to feel like this knowing we were only feeling like this together. My poor Jay, he was sweating a bit lost for words. I knew what he was getting at and I eased my body into his and simply said yes. We were now monogamous; Just as I was about to kiss Jay, we stopped at the 6th floor. A woman, who initially didn't strike me as anyone significant, boarded and pressed 7, our floor. Then, she turned to us, perhaps trying to be polite, and let out that familiar laugh of hers. "Hey?" Jay said, his voice trembling slightly, as if it had cracked a bit. She looked directly at me and flashed the biggest, toothy smile, her lips painted red.

My cheeks flushed, and Jay and I, unfortunately, moved apart.

*Shit. Shit. Shit.*

*Her?*

*Why on God's green earth is she here all dolled up, laughing like an idiot? No one told a joke.*

"B?" Jay quivers her name as his voice breaks.

My heart begins racing, and I want the earth to swallow me whole. *The last thing I wanted was to be caught by my boss.*

The elevator dings, and I am in a hurry.

*That woman could ruin anything.*

I sigh, swiping my card to unlock the door.

I step in and excuse myself, but I don't disappear too far into the bedroom. I hear faint conversations from the other end of the hall, and I have a clear view of them. My eyes sting at the sight of her.

I can see that Barbara is happily chit-chatting with her sing-songy voice.

*Can't help but eavesdrop, can you? Feeling a bit insecure that you can't keep up?*

Barbara leans into Jay, placing her hands on her hips. "I was just on my way to seduce you… into a business deal, but since the seducing is done…" she smiles maliciously as her words trail off, "we can just get straight to business." Jay seemed a bit taken aback, hurt even. "Is this why you've come to NY?" he questioned… the door creaked at that moment, I scurried out of ear and eye shot. She must've smoothed whatever distaste he seemed to have over because by week's end Jay's company was a newly added client on our roster, kudos to the red lipstick, I guess.

*Her; and her fucking red lips.*

Something snaps me back to where I am lying dead to the world—cold, hungover, curled up in my bed. Though the lingering smell of the Chinese food that isn't actually in front of me is still there. Chinese food was my mom's cure. If she had one too many glasses of wine it was Chinese and cola the next day, if Dad had pissed her off and not come home the 100th time they had gotten back together since the initial break up when I was 3, it was wine and Chinese. I was a lot like my mother growing up, meek and lacking confidence, too quiet when I should've spoken up, letting myself get swallowed by dark feelings especially when a woman who was her polar opposite stole my father from under her. That's how my mom will tell me she stole him. I see it otherwise now. She allowed it; my mother simply allowed it. I don't allow such things. Not anymore. Being like my mother didn't sit well with me. College is when I decided enough of that, it was like looking in the mirror my mother and I, so I dyed my tresses dark, got into working out and realized my looks and this multifaceted brain of mine were my biggest asset. As soon as I graduated, I played to my dad's guilt from not raising me in the same household. I still feel kind of bad about that; he's a great father, but I needed access to money and freedom and a little clout from his established business and mostly I needed escape from my mother's overbearing ways so I got my father to vouch for me as a former employee of his for my resume.

My mom pressed my dad for some time about convincing me to see someone for ADHD throughout HS. Sure, I had a tantrum or two. I was used to getting my way so when I didn't, I may not have acted in good taste. My little episodes always caused my mother to overreact and call me "crazy" and say, "I'm off my meds." That's a term people use. I'm not actually on any meds. I digress. My mother is the reason I dyed my hair dark. The siren who bewitched *him* is the reason I keep it dark.

The phone is illuminating; it's Jay. "Hello... babe?" I say.

The noise at his end reaches my ears and all I hear is muffled static whirring.

After failed attempts to yell hello, I no longer have the energy to continue the call. I hang up the phone, and my will to stay awake diminishes just like my appetite. I grab a handful of my hair and pull it forward, the colors fading. I imagine my roots are my mother's hue. Explained a lot. I'm not looking my best so I'm not feeling myself. I'll need to take care of this later. I'm annoyed with myself. When did I give Barbara so much power? I run my fingers through my hair; a strand catches on the center stone of my ring and I sigh and close my eyes.

# CHAPTER 4

# ENGAGEMENT AND CHILDREN

It's been six months since Jay and I have been officially together as a couple. Last night, he got down on one knee and proposed to me. He made sure that we were surrounded by our family and friends before he went ahead with his plans to put a ring on it. My parents, his parents, and all our friends were present with us.

*Friends, haha. You barely have any.*

*Your one and only lovely boss… friend, Barbara.*

I always admired Barbara, it wasn't news that I was fascinated by her work ethic and her appearance.

*De Ja Vu.*

I would have considered her worthy of being my friend, until things took a turn once Jay entered the picture.

Barbara would become an exaggerated version of herself when she was in Jay's presence. It was as if her personality shifted entirely to garner his attention. For the longest time, I didn't understand why she was setting her sights on Jay knowing he was spoken for. It's like she was gunning for me.

*Don't flatter yourself. If she wanted Jay, she would take him. It has nothing to do with you.*

*It has everything to do with you if you'd just wake up you'd see.*

*She wants him for herself. I am sure of it.*

Her demeanor lately made my stomach coil. Why couldn't she back off? Why does she always want to reverse the attention to her when I am getting just a little bit of shine? The shine that I deserve might I add.

Last night, at our surprise engagement, Jay rented out an exquisite bar near the stadium. He rented it out for the night and had a talented pianist serenade us throughout the evening by playing all of our favorite songs. Towards the left side of the bar's entrance was a grand table decorated with a few floral arrangements, delectable sweets, and gourmet tapas. Everything was so perfect until the bartender walked in and transported me to a place of doubt. I guess, after six months of being together, the least I expected from Jay was to remember that whiskey wasn't my drink of choice. It was supposed to be my night in every way, and this was a cool reminder that he doesn't know me nearly as well enough as he should.

I shrugged the annoyance away, reminding myself that after all, men would always be men.

I was in the middle of shoving a buffalo chicken empanada bite in my mouth when the bartender brought out the last decanter, walking slowly as he placed it on the table before me. I noticed it was filled with an amber liquid, which caused my eyes to roll internally. The decanter was engraved in gold, right at the center of the elegant vessel it read: Mrs. James.

I was always amused by the fact that Jay had two first names, and his last name was cute when it was paired with mine, but wait, was this actually happening? Was it all coming to gather as it should? My heart raced as I began to comprehend the name on the decanter, the title along with it... *Mrs. James.* I couldn't believe my eyes. I almost read the name four times, and then I glanced around quickly, trying to look for Jay.

When I turned around, he was on one knee.

He gave a love-laced speech about how I kept him guessing through the past few months, that with me, life was never boring, and he would never let me forget "me" in the chaos that life had to offer. Everything blurred, and the room started spinning when I heard him say, "I love you. Will you please make me the happiest and probably craziest man on this and marry me?" I immediately said yes and to my surprise, crawling out from the crevices of the bar were our family and friends!

*Oh, and Barbara.*

After the initial sting of her presence, I barely noticed her. I was too busy ogling at my two-carat emerald-cut solitaire ring and the handsome man working the room that had just put it on my finger.

I felt as if I was on cloud nine. I can't recall a time when I was this genuinely happy. This moment may have surpassed the moment I met *him.* I busied myself mingling and chatting around, smiling as the sound of glasses clinking together filled the air.

Out of the blue, my eyes met Barbara's. Despite evading her gaze all night, she gestured for me to join her. With a deep breath, I approached her, and together, we quietly withdrew from the crowd. She said she just wanted to check in and ask me if I was doing alright. She reminded me that she was aware that I barely had any other friends apart from her. Looked like the guilt of not "watching out" for me was eating her up.

She smiled at me but her eyes seemed cold.

*As if I needed her jealousy-filled opinion or her trash check-ins on my personal life.*

I know we had friendly chats before, but I was sure that this stance of hers was a ploy against me. I could feel the envy radiating from her. She went on and on about whether I was truly ready to move on. Saying how good of a guy Jay was, as if this was news to me. She was continuously advising me to take my time so Jay didn't end up being my rebound.

*Is it delusion, drugs? Why she thinks she has the place to comment on this is beyond me.*

*Is there a chance she truly thinks we are friends? Am I the crazy asshole?*

I may have overshared a time or two, but that was only because Barbara and I would usually catch up with each other at happy hour. Me drinking wine and her a Jameson neat, losing our minds. But being chatty with her didn't mean she had an opening to hand out her unsolicited opinions on my life. Hell, after a few glasses of wine I was chatty with the walls and they hardly responded.

It was none of her business to be concerned with whether or not I was over my ex. I could sense it. She just wanted Jay for herself.

*She was trying to gaslight me into changing my mind.*

*On the day of my engagement.*

*Bitch.*

But I resigned with the knowledge that he wanted me. I thanked her for checking in, gave her the phoniest smile, and winked her goodbye.

*Oh, Barbara, you are see-through, you're lying and I am, too.*

*If only you could see.*

It was time for me to return to my celebration, but before I could, I nearly jumped out of my body when a large, warm hand grazed my back and softly whispered in my ear, asking if I was okay. It was Jay, of course, and he looked concerned.

He said I seemed flustered, standing secluded in the corner as if I'd just walked in on a ghost. I giggled at his choice of words and kissed his cheek to reassure him that I was okay. I looked over at Barbara and tightened my grip on his arm.

*Mine.*

Before I knew it, my mom rushed towards me, waving in excitement as she pulled me in a hug. That was the exact moment Barbara jumped in to congratulate Jay. He smiled and nodded happily while keeping his eyes on me before I turned away. I was surely about to pop a blood vessel in my neck from the restraint I was using not to look their way. At that moment, it seemed the universe knew I needed a distraction. I got an overwhelming whiff of Coco Chanel and turned towards the scent.

To my right was that familiar auburn-haired woman sitting at the bar, staring at Jay and Barbara. Oh, I never wanted to be somebody else so badly.

Before my body could catch up to what my brain wanted to do, which was approach this woman, my father spun me into a hug. When he let me go, my mom was fluttering away, chatting up Jay's mom and I scanned the room to look for her again.

"Dad, do you know who the woman who was sitting just over there is?" I asked him, looking in the direction she was just in.

"Probably one of your mother's friends. You know how she is." he replied, seemingly uninterested.

I retreated with a nod; he was probably right. It must have been a coincidence, but I couldn't stop thinking I had seen her somewhere before. Our party was ending, and the last four remaining people were our parents. Jay and I thanked everyone for celebrating with us, and before bidding them all goodnight, we made plans with Jay's parents for breakfast.Jay and I stepped out into the evening air, my fingers intertwined with his. "So, fiancé, your place or mine?" I said, staring up at him doe-eyed. "Mine. I mean ours… Mrs. James. I want to put an offer on that house you loved last month. I've been canvassing the neighbors and it's still on the market and honestly, I love it too. But for now, let's just consider the condo our place. What's mine is yours, babe." he replied, caressing my face.

I didn't think it was possible to love Jay to a point where I would ever be able to erase *him* from my memory, but that night, I could see it happening. I could feel myself melting in his presence. *Maybe I wouldn't need to be her anymore.* I got on my tippy toes to kiss him, and the lights from the busy street illuminated the tinges of red in his hair, making me lose my senses. I kissed him deeply, and he gripped my waist tighter with each kiss.I was eager to go to his, *our* place, but to my disappointment, flashbacks of my conversations with Barbara replayed in my head.

*Was I ready to move on? What if she was right, and I was hurrying myself into a risky future? What if I hadn't covered all bases.*

I knew I wouldn't see my ex again; he made sure of that. He also made sure to leave the marks of his existence engraved on my soul because he was selfish. Sure, I loved *him,* but he didn't love me enough to stay and that solidified why Jay is the man I am meant to be with.

Why shouldn't I move on? Why can't I be selfish like *him?*

*You know it's him you see when the mint hue of Jay's eyes turn a fiery green.*

*You know he's the one you're imagining when you're kneeling in front of Jay ready to swallow every ounce of him.*

My intruding thoughts make me sick.

Just because I see *his* green eyes when I look into Jay's doesn't mean I don't love Jay.

*It is normal to think of your ex when your fiancé is tangled up with you in bed, kissing you? Right?*

Barbara doesn't know what she's talking about.

*Barbara should mind her own fucking business.*

*Bar...*

"Babe? Where'd you go?" Jay snapped me out of my thoughts, and I realized we were somehow lying on the couch. I didn't even remember the walk home.

"I'm here," I said as I smiled weakly. "Just tired from the most amazing night."

"Rest, love." He gently kissed my forehead.

*Fucking Barbara.*

*Fucking, fucking, bitch.*

I screamed in my head, and the thoughts cascaded down into my veins; I felt as if it was taking everything in me to not explode. My body was collapsing from the pain.

I closed my eyes and turned my face away from Jay's.

It is my freaking night. My fiance's dick should be stabbing the back of my throat right now, but that bitch has flooded my thoughts with guilt and killed my entire mood.

But rest I shall.

I have been extremely tired lately; my appetite is all over the place, and I'm constantly thirsty. My moods haven't been very even; to top it off, my mother tells me it's nothing new.

She can't judge my character, given how she is. If I was left to her, and my dad wasn't around, she would have had me in a looney bin. I remember the day I stood in the bathroom as I took the pregnancy test. The strip showed two double pink lines. Because I couldn't believe the first one, three more sticks and three more blue plus signs later I was clearly pregnant. I remember being a mixed bag of emotions, all of them erupting inside my chest. Happy, scared, but mostly boastful. I could not wait to rub it in my mother's face that my mood swings were caused by the fact that a tiny human was growing inside of me. She, being a woman and mother failed to even notice that.

I wanted to tell her that this isn't the high school me, and I am not a hormonal maniac. That she doesn't need to worry. I could do this.

*Yeah, my tantrums have indeed continued into adulthood from time to time, but this was a win for me.*

Jay's reaction to becoming a father left me in awe. He was planning the nursery and already looking at schools for our little unborn sweet pea. It was times like these that made me almost forget *him.*

My mother was smiling ear to ear when we FaceTimed her to break the news after we hit thirteen weeks. Her eyes, however, looked like her nightmares had come true. Sadly, my eyes probably read the same. This meant she'd be around more, maybe pushing her agenda, maybe smothering me out of concern under the premise of love. I was getting ahead of myself with these concerns unfortunately neither of us would need them. My dad was so pumped he kept calling my unborn son his bambino, and Jay's parents were joyful. They said this is just the kind of news they needed. Jay's parents and I were good. We got along fine, but they lived on the West Coast in California, so our bond was more surface level than I would prefer. I understood though they couldn't bear to stay here with constant reminders of their deceased son. I could see their pain. I felt that sort of pain, too. They deserve forgiveness.

When I told Barbara that I was about to become a mom, she looked pleased, but her congratulations dripped with disgust.

*I am sure she didn't like children. She thought of them to be in her way. A matter of constant inconvenience.*

Being pregnant had its perks; working at the office became easier because my workload declined to half.

Barbara would tease me, indicating that I was of no use to her in the field now with my swollen belly. Well, she was right; I couldn't exactly attract men with a baby growing inside of me. I know some men have a fetish for that sort of thing but I wasn't keen on it.

The blood test results came back; we were having a boy. I think Jay must've leaped ten feet off the ground. He was so excited. My pregnancy was easy for the most part until it wasn't. There was no trauma, no blood, and no baby.

*No baby.*

I couldn't tell you what happened to my son if I wanted to. It's like it didn't happen to me. Like I wasn't even there. I hear them talking. Barbara says I've blocked it. That I'm likely suffering from PTSD. She's probably right. I can't recall anything. No one talked about it with me. I know it must've been something because I had a short hospital stay that did more damage than good. In a nutshell I had to be sedated given my phobia of hospitals, that is. Of course, being sedated doesn't really help your stream of consciousness.

The following pregnancy was the same, the next being a girl. Another child that didn't come to fruition. Deep down I begged for her, pleaded with God not to punish me with her. I wanted to be everything for her that I needed. I needed to be everything to her. But there were other plans for me. Our house still had their rooms made up. We put a lot of thought into their rooms, the type of atmosphere we wanted our children surrounded with. Couldn't bring myself to take them apart. Perhaps I should revisit their rooms again; leaving them untouched isn't solving anything. But not today.

We had been trying and I had been failing ever since. My Jay, however, though I am sure he's riddled with hurt, anger, grief and disappointment, he's still been so supportive. He hasn't blamed me for anything. In fact no one has made an issue of my failure to carry to full term. I assume they don't want to trigger me for my sake and cause another hospital trip. So they let me live inside my delusional walls where nothing is wrong. I constantly think about it, but I'd never bring it up—too much shame. *It's just forty weeks. I can't seem to keep them in me.*

I don't know what the issue is. I guess I should've seen a therapist to talk through the emotions because I've blocked it all out or worked up the courage to call my OB— so she could tell me exactly what went wrong but instead, I took solace in venting to Barbara.

As overbearing and intrusive as she was sometimes it also gave way to the fact that Barbara knew me pretty well, and so I went to her. If she said something I didn't want to hear I could further justify my case against her, and if she said something that seemed like she was a little too involved I could justify the case in my head that she was in fact getting too close for comfort. When I confided in her, Barbara reassured me that when things are meant to be they will be. She said children aren't a part of this chapter and to forget them for now and move on, that I was strong and needn't let this weigh on me. That I had other things to focus on and when it was time to get reacquainted with my children, I would choose it and do it on my terms.

So I blocked my children out and I tried to recenter myself.

I don't know why I confided in her. My love-hate relationship with her is very confusing; it still makes my head spin.I had taken Barbara's advice once before at a very pivotal moment in my life and that advice was the best thing I have ever done. Listening to her again didn't seem too far-fetched.

# CHAPTER 5

# GONE WITH THE CHILDREN

I've been in bed for so long that I don't know where the bed begins and my body ends. It's possible this mattress that I've grown to know so well is embedded with rocks or maybe we were scammed, and it's an old school spring mattress as opposed to the memory foam we thought we purchased. My body feels like the day after you've run a marathon that you did not train for. You can't sit, can't stand, can't bend without a constant throbbing, and forget about doing any of those at a normal human pace you're moving at geriatric double hip replacement pace. I am talking bone deep throbbing.

As miserable as the aching of my body is, the drowned-out sound of beeping is what really interrupts my semi-slumber; my arms scream at me as I attempt to roll over. This time, I don't even have the energy to open my eyes. I don't have the will power either.

The beeps are muffled, the sound from some reality show is fading out, and I feel as if I am submerged six feet deep underwater. Every noise is a faint whisper, and it is defying reason at this point.

I want to get up and turn the TV off, or m*aybe I want to break it so it shuts up permanently, tomatoe, tomato...*

But frankly, I am lazy and unsuccessfully trying to sleep it off. I don't want to move an inch from my bed; I just want to sleep, especially now. Remembering my failed pregnancies isn't high on my list of favorite things to do, and I would go to the ends of the earth to avoid ever having to remember them. I know this is in part why I've distanced myself from everyone, mostly Leigh. Leigh is a good friend, but she is also a stark reminder that unlike me, she's a mother to Aaron and Alivia. A damn good one from what I can tell.

*And what I am is years of misery and failure.*

*A failed mother. I could have been in her shoes, living her life, but I'm not.*

*I'm not her.*

So I don't want to be around Leigh. I want to, but I guess I can't stand to be with them, not for long because then the thoughts come crashing in and taking everything in its path with it like a tsunami. They engulf me whole.

Then I will cling to everything I see before me in Leigh's life that is a grave reminder of what could've been and I simply cannot take that. It makes me uncomfortable in my own skin, so much so that my brain is trying to claw its way out. I envy her and at times I even hate her so naturally I've pushed her away so I don't have to live in the shadows of wanting what she had.

I have a hard time admitting when my mind has reached capacity. I don't seek help when I should so of course, none of it has been easy on my mental health, and instead of going to a therapist, I ran to Barbara. We are so alike when we need to get things done, so it felt safe to vent to her. I needed someone to shake me and kick my ass in gear.

*Because you're weak and can't do it on your own, can you?*

Barbara suggested I move on and block it. Well, I don't know if it's a good or bad thing, but I've blocked almost all of it.I neatly put everything in a box and pushed it inside the attic of my head.

**List of things I shouldn't visit:**

*My OB*

*My Therapist*

*People with children*

*The Weaker Versions of Myself*

I blocked any and everything that could be a trigger.

My body aches, and I don't feel like I will be able to get comfortable enough to sleep deeply anymore. I assume it's better if I at least try to get up and face life; maybe then this beeping will stop. The discomfort seems all too familiar, and I don't want to sit in it. I can't sit in it. It is crippling for me, it's sterile, it's bland, it's gray, and at times it's Jay. Sometimes, my husband makes me so uncomfortable with his planning, cleanliness, staple gray, navy black suits. His always manicured hair never a strand out of place. His tone, oh his tone, it never changes. He never yells, he's never overly excited, his laugh is even calm. It makes me yearn for more, it makes me remember things I want to forget.

His condo did that to me, too. It made my skin crawl. But back then I wasn't in the same position I am now. I still had to make him wholly mine so I persevered; I don't think I have it in me to power through the way I used to.I shouldn't have to. He should be what I need him to be. I know he sees it; the difference in me when he lets his spark come through. But then he puts it out; he'd rather live in the gray.

I was never comfortable in the gray; it served as a window to a place I wanted to forget. I wanted it all erased from my memory, but the more I tried, the more I remembered.

*You can only bury it so far down until it breaks through to the other side.*

I had tried my best to spice it up to add warmth and a dash of color. I tried to start a fire, but nothing I did made me feel any less cold when I was at his place. I battered him for weeks about it. I pushed for his input, I would've been happier with a "that's fucking hideous" and a bit of elevation to his voice, but he just brushed it off. He asked me not to worry about it too much. After all, we were going to get married and we were about to move anyway. He was right; a little patience could help. But a little fire could, too.

*You used to be so patient.*

We were touring homes, and we put an offer in on the house that I loved with our realtor just four weeks before Jay went down on one knee, asking me to be his wife. I didn't know it would be our home when we were looking, but something about it screamed at me. It had rose bushes lining the front porch, a porch big enough for a swing. A huge red maple tree that had glossy red and orange leaves. The house itself was white with black shutters and red brick accents; it was straight out of a how to make your home rich magazine. The tree house in the backyard tugged at my heart strings which didn't quite feel natural, sometimes it all depended on my mood.

We have a delayed closing for our beautiful 4-bedroom 3-bath home that sits in a cul-de-sac because the seller is going through a nasty divorce, which is unfortunate for them, but why is that my problem? Am I supposed to wait thirty more days until I feel at ease?

There's only one photo that radiates in the living room of the condo and it is of my love. It's obviously from happier times before the harsh world took over and washed him gray. He wore blue jeans, sandals, and an afghan looking like an adventure in human form. I get tingles looking at that photo, but it's not the same when I'm looking at Jay in person. I'm beginning to think it's Jay's presence now that is dimming my world. If I stare at the photo long enough, I feel my throat closing up. The man in the image isn't the man I get every day. *Who in their right mind could live like this? In limbo.*

I've tried painting the walls to make this house more interesting, climbed on the sofas to hang different floral arrangements, and drilled a few frames. I even bought a velvet green sofa with the perfect balance of emerald and Kelly green. I just wanted to wash this bleakness out. I needed some warmth to penetrate me like just the mere presence of *him* had. I needed it to surround me and soothe me when Jay couldn't. Anything to fill the void.

So, I hung an abstract portrait of naked bodies, three women painted in browns and terracotta over our bed. Jay thought it was gaudy because our tastes don't match, but oh well. It is what it is. I thought it was profound that the artist titled the work "Love them all" and there are just so many ways you can interpret this;

3 women so different yet the same.

Jay has been working day and night, and the bags under his eyes tell me he's tired. The bags that remain packed tell me he's leaving again. The draft is approaching closer and closer, and he is in demand. I get it.

*I guess the least he can do is put up with my freaking velvet green couch. He winces, and I smile. In my eyes, it's a fair deal.*

He tries to hide the fact that he grimaces every time he sees my eclectic displays of décor. I don't believe in symmetry, symmetry is boring. Things don't have to match, and you can find great things if you look just beyond the chaos. I try to tone it down, but I can't help it. It gives me immense pleasure to see him uncomfortable. Others have had to live with that feeling, he should, too. I mean he's made me uncomfortable. I've taken it in stride.

Don't get me wrong, I love Jay so purposefully making him uncomfortable and enjoying it is a maddening feeling. It's almost like I need to make sure we must be a little unhappy to prove to *him* that I am eternally his.

*And Jay has no other choice. We were destined.*

I only know I've come up from another memory because I can hear someone murmuring in my ear, and I can't figure out what they are saying. My thoughts and their voices fuse, and I don't know whom to hear anymore. Goosebumps send chills down my spine, and I am continuously slipping in and out of a loop. I feel dizzy from being in this dream-like state. I am almost nauseous, almost awake, almost asleep. I am almost everything at once yet, I am never here.

I am breathing in and out of memories all day. It's a limbo of consciousness so I've decided that whatever grapes Treehouse uses in their wines, they may need to check the orchard for a rogue plant because what the fuck.

*Weed? Shrooms? Berries?*

*Denial?*

I am no saint. I have dabbled in some illegal substances; I have also been prescribed a medicine or two, so I think I have cause to question Treehouse. I tried magic shrooms with Barbara when I was fresh out of graduate school. I had just landed this gig, and Barbara invited me to an industry party. I was in my element and ultimately feeding off of her energy; she was a badass, commanding the attention of practically everyone.

That night, she reminded me of *him* and the day we first met. I probably would've jumped off a bridge if she said to that night, she was just that mesmerizing. I would've crawled through the fire if he said to, he was a man who commanded the room just by entering it. If he looked in your direction, it made you feel as if you were the only two people in the room. If he looked away from you, he'd take your breath with him. He caused that kind of a frenzy of excitement and that's exactly what she was doing.

*He'd be proud.*

Barbara starts giving me the eye periodically; when I finally catch the hint I discreetly follow her lead. She leads us to a secluded area of the event space and we ducked off into the bathroom midway through the night. We stumbled in laughing and giving each other high fives. We were both at our professional best. The champagne had been flowing all night so it was nice to escape in there for a few minutes and just relax. We both knew it was a successful night, so to celebrate, Barbara whipped out a little baggie. I hid the look of confusion on my face and tried my best to mask my hesitation, but she insisted and I couldn't turn her down.Now I never knew shrooms came in powdered form, but you learn something new every day and I snorted that shit like babe pig in the city and let it spread its magic through my veins. Barbara was laughing obnoxiously at my shake rattle and roll post snort. Not like I sniffed mushrooms in my spare time on the regular. So, my body reacted like you do when you get a shiver out of nowhere. She did her thing and while I waited for her to finish primping, I did a quick mirror check and lipstick reapplication before we headed back out to rejoin the festivities.

Now I can't tell you exactly when I lost all recollection of time and space but I did. The most vivid memory I have was being through the fucking moon happy. I was excitedly pitching our products to the fish tank. In their language. Use your imagination on exactly what fish language sounds like. I had been inquiring about Nemo and practically fucking singing until my voice was hoarse, terribly dancing till I felt my heels would break off from my ankles buckling so much, but the worst of it was that I was aware of what I was doing, I just didn't care. I didn't realize talking to the fish wasn't a reasonable thing to be doing at the time, but I knew I was talking to them.

It was only when I saw Barbara glaring at me that I paused. She was whispering to the men next to her, staring at me without blinking. *What the fuck was wrong with her? It was her idea to do shrooms, not mine. Why the hell was she not singing to the fishes with me? She took the shrooms, and I saw it.*

I kid you not; she snorted the entire thing in a single sniff. A regular professional.

So why am I standing here like an idiot in shock while she's looking pristine and completely sober as if she hadn't had a single drink all night nonetheless? Barbara was perfectly fine meanwhile my brain thought I was starring in Cirque Du Soleil. This obviously did not add up. It was a very sobering moment when Barbara barely smiled at me, as she walked away, breaking her gaze. She seemed content and, perhaps, even a bit disturbed by me. But more so relieved that she could turn away and rid herself of having to deal with me at all. Barbara could turn away and not look back and completely forget I existed.

It was that night that I knew I had to keep her close. She must've set me up. She didn't like that I was doing well without summoning her, she needed to knock me down a notch. Whether Barbara was my friend or my enemy—was to be determined. I would be in pursuit of clarity and our existence would either solidify or crumble.

****

I should call Jay again to see if he finally has better service. I pick up the phone and swipe up to call him; it takes little to no effort since his contact is pinned at the top. He answers immediately, and I can hear his voice albeit very low. Jay is talking to someone, and he sounds empathetic. Oh, no, he almost sounds serious, but I can't make out the words. I'm pressing my ear to the phone screen so hard that it hurts. It's pissing me off that I can't make out what he's saying, not that I don't trust him, it's just I am nosey, okay?

*Don't trust him? You shouldn't trust yourself.*

And the tone in his voice is making the hair on my arms stand up. Jay is not the one for emotions so to hear his voice so raw has my head spinning even harder than it already has been. Suddenly, there's a loud slamming of doors, the sound regurgitates so loudly it's like I slammed the door myself. I hear glass crackle and split slowly which hurls me to my feet.

I'm dizzy when I stand up, but I don't have the time to think about it much. I had to figure out what was happening. My heart raced, and a lump formed in my throat, signaling that something was very wrong.

The phone is still pressed to my ear lightly. I take a few steps, and now I'm frantically peering through the glass window of my bedroom. I see my neighbors. Leigh, her husband, and her kids. Their kids are calmly being strapped into their car seats by their dad while Leigh stands looking on shifting her weight from one foot to the other. Her husband gently closes the rear door and walks around into Leigh's hand, that is holding onto the driver's side car door handle looking up at him with pleading eyes.

Her husband's face is unreadable—it's not anger, no, it's sadness mixed with confusion. He says a few words that seem to strike Leigh because of the way her chest just caved in and he turns away from her and gets into the car. Leigh reaches for his shirt, but he gently swipes it away out of her grasp. This scene feels familiar to me, maybe because Jay and I aren't in the best of positions either and Leigh is my friend so I can relate to her, but still this is wrong. I shouldn't have a front row seat to something this vulnerable. *Thank you, moral compass, for being captain obvious.*

I am stuck now trying to dissect the scene before me, wondering what went wrong. Then I noticed her. My auburn-haired friend with the weight of the world in her eyes.

*Friend?*

Leigh stares up at me, and I am frozen near the window, trying to read her, but her expression is equally blank. But her eyes, her eyes are yelling. She looks like she needs to tell me something. As if the silence will eat her alive; if she doesn't convey it, she will probably suffocate. She's always looked like this even when I didn't know her the way I do now.

*Strange.*

I've seen her roaming around in the city numerous times. I remember catching a glimpse of her at the bar, at the market, out on the street. I guess she's got one of those familiar, neutral faces, so neutral that it's a bit eerie.

*It's not just a familiar face if you know the face.*

I'm still looking at her from my window, and the phone's still glued to my ears. I almost forget about it until laughter erupts from the other end of the cell, and my blood boils. My throat starts to burn, and I can feel the nausea building up from hearing her voice.

*That fucking laugh is piercing.*

"JAY?! WHY ARE YOU WITH BARBARA!" I yell into the phone, my hands shaking.

The lines immediately disconnect.

I pace back and forth and stare out at the window.

*What THE hell?*

My friend, Leigh, is holding the phone in her hands, still standing in her driveway looking up at me with sadness. I don't know what is happening anymore, but something isn't right. I begin to pinch myself because if I'm stuck in another dream I want out. I want my body to move, I want to go out there and check on Leigh, but I just can't. I'm hanging on by a thread, and my internal turmoil is ripening.

*All thanks to Barbara.*

I turn away from the window and draw my attention back to my phone, dialing Jay as he picks up.

"What the hell is going on? Care to explain?" I yell again.

"Babe… I love you." he says so calmly and my entire system feels like it's malfunctioning.

"Don't play coy with me, why is Barbara there?" I said. "Explain why Barbara is there," I repeat with emphasis, I feel sick.

*You are sick.*

Instead of giving me the clarity I need, he ignores my plea and continues to talk, going on and on about how he works too much, that he's going to change, that he needs me, that I complete the puzzle of our family. Yada yada.

*Yeah, right.*

I scoff because surely me and the painting on the wall can't be the family he's talking about.

Jay's still eating my head off with his useless nonsense, but then we are interrupted again.

Video call from Barbara.

*What the fuck is going on today?*

I don't even put Jay on hold before I go to answer her call. By now, my face has turned red, and my eyes are welling up with frustration. My hands are visibly shaking, and my ears are hot. I answer with venom in my voice and immediately ask her what she thinks she's doing with my husband. She looks so perplexed and amused that she starts to laugh.

*Oh. God. No.*

I can see her background and wherever she is looks similar to my study's décor. She said she has no idea what the fuck I'm on about.

*Did I picture her laughing in my head and then willed myself to hear it?*

*No, you couldn't have. You were looking at Leigh and talking to Jay, that makes no sense.*

I go to speak, but she smiles with her red lips into the screen and her words brush past mine so effortlessly making me feel small in my space.

She starts gushing about how my performance is suffering because lately, I've only been catering to my husband and whatever the hell I am obsessed with now. "People will start to notice," she says. "And trust me, you don't want that," she reiterates. She ends with the most insightful constructive criticism and that is simply that I need to get my shit together.

*Yeah, I would if only you would leave me alone!*

I never know which version of her I'm going to get: the raging bitch, the friend, the boss.

*The I'll flirt with your man in front of you, cunt.*

*Maybe, that. Mostly, that.*

I reassure her it's just market saturation, that I'm on top of things, and that we really would have discussed this at the office. She told me I've been on her mind and it was time for her to check in on me.

*Yeah, I'm not dumb.*

She's about to end this pleasant call but pauses and says, "You know, Jay will never fill the void of *him.* Once you accept that, the better you will be."

I abruptly end that check in and slam her back outside of my thoughts.

*Fucking hell.*

She didn't want to discuss work with me. She had ulterior motives to get inside my head. She's good at trying to tear me down under the façade of being my friend. My biggest mistake was considering her a friend and letting her in my life. She knows too much about me.

I am in a vulnerable state, and she's enjoying playing games.

*I am not in love with my ex. I am not.*

*I am married to Jay. We are starting a family.*

*Everything is okay.*

*She's obsessing over my ex, not me.*

*Not me. It's her.*

Barbara is so cunning that she's holding this knowledge over my head, dangling it like a carrot. No surprise there; she knows what *he* was to me. It's as if she's warning me, subtly threatening to tell my husband I haven't moved on.

She just wants to sink her teeth into him.

She's purposefully tried to infest my married life with doubts. I've got to distance myself and my Jay from her before she does something I can't reverse.

I call Jay back once Barbara's out of sight, but he doesn't answer. I try a few times before I decide to leave him a voicemail that says, "I love you." Clicking my phone shut, I peer out the window again, but my neighbors are gone.

*Note to self:*

*Call and check on Leigh.*

I'm certain she wanted to tell me something before someone barged in to fuck with my psyche.

My lovely neighbor has been a somber voice of reason for me plenty of times, always there at the right moment when my mind begins to frazzle.

I would say I'm pretty high-strung, so it's nice to have someone around who brings out a different side of you. We could probably use each other's company right now, but she isn't here.

The phone dings, and it's a text from my mom. "Please, honey bee." It reads.

I roll my eyes and get to bed.

"Not right now, Mom." I sigh.

*I am not ready yet.*

# MIRRORED WORDS

I am rubbing my temples with my thumb and pointer fingers trying to calm my nerves, and stop the stabbing feeling that has only intensified. Barbara's little drop in has put me on edge, and I can't stop my eye from drifting over to the wine rack and catching the treehouse vineyards cabernet, and after a very short internal deliberation I pour two glasses and call Leigh. Because isn't the saying you have to bite the dog that bit you or something like that. Plus, this is cabernet not merlot so I'm already off to a better start. She arrives before I even finish inviting her. She's got this sixth sense about her. Eerie at times. When Leigh arrives, I embrace her. Her hugs are always so light and warm; her presence is comforting so it makes up for the lack of physicality. I rambled a bit about how I'm having quite the day as I led her to my study with its bright red walls and the green velvet couch I bought that my husband despised. I still love when he winces at the sight of it.

Leigh enters the room like she's floating on air. Her aura seems so light despite whatever it was I witnessed earlier. I admire that about Leigh, she's like the calm in the storm like a lighthouse. As many times as she's been inside of my study, she's never looked jarred by my taste in decor and I've never thought to question it until today. She doesn't look completely at ease; she keeps staring at the walls and fixing her shit that isn't out of place. She's fidgeting. It's a bit alarming given her usual composure. She's one of those people who can endure discomfort, who can push through it; she's stronger than I am in that regard. However, the slight tension in her eyes and the hint of stiffness in her shoulders let me know that something is troubling her. I have always been very keen on things. I am a watcher. It's what I do, I study people and things and react accordingly.

"Sit." I say as I pat the space beside me on the couch and scoot back to sit Indian style while turning to face my friend. She sits and turns her knees toward me and leans in a tad. This look of discomfort seems to have nothing to do with my decor and everything to do with whatever is the matter. I think it must be about what I saw and judging by the weight in her stiff shoulders it is heavy, poor Leigh.

I know she won't break the ice, so I lay a hand on her thigh and I start.

"I noticed the commotion between you and your husband.

You know me and I don't mean to pry, but is everything alright?" I pause a breath and continue, "I know I've been a bit distant, but I am still here, if you were to ever need me, to talk or to just grab a bite, you know how to reach me, right?" She takes a deep breath and begins by saying, "No, I am finding it harder to reach you lately, you're so close yet you're so far." Sometimes, the way Leigh phrases things catches me off guard. They're odd, almost too intimate for the situation. I usually chalk it up to her quirkiness, but my gut is telling me there's something I am missing about my friend Leigh.

I see her mouth moving and her eyebrows are bouncing up and down matching the emotion on her face. I hear sounds. I'm listening, but I am too distracted by my own staring. I'm entranced. I don't even think I'm blinking as I look at her much like I have in the past. I saw her the night I met Jay at the bar and I saw her at my engagement party as well. It all clicked when we had finally moved in and formally introduced ourselves. I couldn't explain why she looked familiar at the bar. I don't believe Jay started canvasing the neighbors on our first time viewing the house. I don't remember anyone being outside, but my memory isn't always the most reliable. As I look at Leigh, I just nod my head not in agreement to what she's saying but in acknowledgement of her. She's always had this face, this familiar knowing welcoming face. I knew she looked familiar back then and that I just couldn't place her or connect her to being outside when we toured our home or being at the bar with her husband the first night I took Jay home.

I later found out her husband and Jay had struck up a friendship and Jay had invited them to our engagement party which explained her presence at that time when I didn't know her at all.I had forgotten about the woman who caught my attention that night because Barbara had infected me with her venomous thoughts.

I wish I had met Leigh that night. I bet my night would've ended differently, her aura was almost ethereal. It was so calming I felt drawn to her. I have the tendency to form attachments and to obsess over minor things probably, so this was no surprise to me. I can't help it. *You could if you were stronger.*

I snap myself back to reality because I don't want her to notice I'm practically drooling at her. Admiration for me is risky business and I don't want my admiration for Leigh to get out of control. It seems I've tuned back in at the right time so as to not appear like some superficial bitch who only invited her over to be nosey and wasn't really listening to her heavy-hearted friend. I mouth a quick, "Thank you," to the universe for divine timing because Leigh was in the middle of confessing something heavy.

She says she's spiraling. She knows she's spiraling; she just can't stop it but she's trying. She doesn't know how else to stop this than to seek help. It's happened to her before, and she gave up before she truly got the help she needed and she is afraid, afraid of leaving and her husband replacing her.

*Odd choice of words, isn't it?*

Through shaky breaths and cracked words, she continues telling me that she feels disconnected from the children. She is so consumed with her internal tug of war that she barely interacts with them and when she remembers them, she doesn't know how to interact with them. Her biggest fear is causing any emotional damage for them so she wills herself to stay away. Her husband is concerned for her, her withdrawal from life is the polar opposite of anything the woman he married would've done. He wants her to get long term help and to wake up right now before it's too late. The kids are afraid to approach her because they never know which mommy they're going to get, and he is afraid to talk to her because she's not receptive to any of his suggestions. She responds in anger or a complete personality switch. He's pleaded with her, he has even gone above and beyond to research doctors and facilities, but on the surface she claims she doesn't want that kind of help. Something in her eyes says she does; she's just afraid to admit it.

I could tell the weight of her emotions were unbearable and she was trying to make sense of the chaos within. I could feel it as if it were happening to me, the air was thick. I recognize all the turmoil I've experienced it before myself, more than once.

There's bravery in acknowledging that your mental health is suffering. I'll give her that. I am happy to give her that. I hope this little fire inside of her that's recognizing things and ready to fight back never dies. Because to be frank, Leigh doesn't exactly scream brave. She doesn't exactly scream anything, she's just Leigh. It's funny how a person could be a morally sound voice, a constant, an actual pillar to lean on for you, but for themselves be nothing. Ironic. I wish I could be better to Leigh. I'm surprised at how close of a friend I considered her. I never expected when she first appeared that I would hear her voice in my head when I was about to make a poor decision, it's truly a testament to the effect she has on me. I know that I haven't been nearly as good to her, and I want to, but every time I try to move in the right direction, Barbara barges in and ruins my mood, time, and energy. She latches onto my skin and drinks the kind selflessness away from me. So unfortunately for Leigh and I, I'm fighting my own battles with this witch, Barbara, and losing. Devoting time elsewhere would be a detriment to me.

I am happy to be here now though drinking it all in. It is obvious Leigh really needed to get this off her chest. The poor thing is leaking like a faucet and singing like a canary and while I am slightly annoyed because she's starting to look and sound like that God awful woman in the gray. The one who was so eager to embrace the process and accept her diagnosis. I remain engaged and I sit in my dimly lit study trying my hardest to be present in this moment, straining my ears and eyes thinking maybe if I open my eyes wider, I'd hear her better. Despite our close proximity her voice is a whisper. She's speaking so softly it's as if she's having a conversation in her mind. My poor friend, all this internal turmoil. When Leigh finally stops talking and looks at me with empty eyes waiting to be filled, anxiously waiting on me to say something truly poetic and insightful that may help or inspire or at the very least be empathetic. I offer her the most generic unhelpful phrase that, "Everything will be okay." I do mean it, though. If things were to turn around and work out for anyone it would be Leigh. I don't encourage getting help because I knew someone who was forced into that kind of "help" before and it didn't bode well for him. I suggest something a bit more of what some would call crunchy or holistic, like meditation and yoga. I suggest that maybe she journal and take note of triggers and re-read her journal at the end of the day, making note of her triggers and right action steps to avoid or manage them in the future. I stole this gem from my past that seemed all too present these days.

Her mention of her husband trying to replace her really struck a chord. It's just such an odd thing to feel I couldn't help but ask her why she thinks he's trying to replace her? She says she can't be sure, it's just a feeling, but the main issue is that they don't have sex like they used to. They've always had a better than average sex life and it's been reduced to nothing and it's concerning. Things that she did that used to turn him on don't anymore, she's afraid someone else is turning his head.

*Tuh, I can relate.*

She said it used to be so feral, so raw and passionate and now he just looks at her as if she will break or worse as if he was afraid of her, afraid to hurt her, afraid to trigger her. He looks at her as if he will ignite a trigger within her that will cause her to explode, hurting him and the children in the wake of it all.

I sigh because the added layer of children must be so difficult to navigate. How can she be everything to everyone and not be sure of herself? I want to sympathize with her and while I'm usually mindful not to dominate conversations, unless I am in work mode. I find myself compelled to share a similar story to convey empathy and connect to Leigh like she's connected to me before so it was nearly impossible for me not to jump in here and let Leigh know she wasn't alone. That she wasn't the only one navigating marital woes.

I blink twice and I begin the blurting of words, "Listen…"

*Smooth opening, Em… wasn't brash or dominating at all.*

"I'm also going through things with Jay. He longs for the type of family I can't give him." She doesn't blink, but raises an eyebrow and smiles weakly. She's amused by that confession or saddened perhaps. I am not sure, I can't read her. This energy puts me off a bit because I find myself guessing at Leigh's sentiment and I don't like to guess.

Leigh puts her head down just for a second before she lifts it again to meet my eyes and just stares at me for what seems like forever and finally gives me an ambiguous smile that conveys more sadness than I think she meant it to. I want to take that sentence back. Her reaction is making me self-conscious and I don't like the pit in my stomach that's just developed at the mention of my family.But Leigh lays a light hand on my shoulder and asks me to go on, so I continue.

"I also have a strong personality, it's complex and I'm certainly not everyone's cup of tea. I still can't believe he chose me sometimes."

*You chose him.*

"I'm successful in my career and that can be intimidating, especially to men. I have a spicier side in the bedroom and our last tryst in the sheets but not actually in the sheets. I may have put him off. I took it too far, it got too dark, I guess..." I preface with, "I'm over sharing I think but c'est la vie." She just nods with half a smile as if to say, "It's a bit too late to stop now, get on with it." So I did.

"Jay had just got home from a business trip. One that went well so his mood was high. He was on the verge of getting one of the top college recruits signed and that was a big win for him. I, on the other hand, had had a particularly rough day. I accepted a potential client pitched to me by my boss. She had been nitpicking my every move the entire day. Questioning if I had our earnings report updated to share. She even questioned if I was due for a trip to the salon. She looked at me so intently. She raked me up and down and I could've sworn I saw a look of disgust in her eyes once her eyes reached the crown of my head where my roots were showing and said, "You know what, maybe I'll just take over everything." She really put emphasis on the term "everything" and I've had my suspicions about her and her intentions with Jay. She's constantly flirtatious. Jay would think me dramatic so I hadn't bothered him with it. Obviously, the way she said "everything" triggered me. So I countered with, "I am the best at pitches. I was holding down the company while you were nowhere to be found, I think I'll be okay." We were at the new building where all our offices were glass. I did not pitch the sale effectively enough and that client did not commit to us. It's one hundred percent Barbara's fault for knocking me off my game, I knew when she said "take over everything" she was talking about more than just this pitch. I could read in between the lines. I am no idiot. Of course, Barbara took the news of my failure hard and berated me loudly and held no punches with the dramatic flair all the while with the office staff peering on. She was so pissed she hurled her whiskey glass at the wall, and it shattered. *The gasps heard around the world,* is what I would call the reaction of the office staff just imagine the sight. My pale complexion and brown liquid spattered about the walls and my shoes, and let us not forget a few drops splashed back from the wall onto my cheeks. I just stood there staring at my feet in silence like an idiot. I don't even remember if Barbara was talking to me afterward, or if she was even still in the office. The next thing I knew was a familiar hand cupping my face and my eyes finally drawing up from the floor to meet my dad's.

My father was in the building that day to take me to lunch, it seems he had impeccable timing. He saw me and pulled me into my office to check on me and calm me down, and said he caught the tail end of the melt down. I heard him talking but my mind was focused on her. I scanned around him, past him, and everywhere for Barbara, who owed me a damn apology with her unprofessional behavior. The nerve of her to act out like that in front of our entire office; I should have reported her to HR. I should've pressed assault charges. I didn't, my one chance to hit her where it would hurt and I just let her walk all over me. The staff whispered as my father and I walked out of the building so that he could drive me home. I was too shaken up and raw with emotion to drive myself according to my doting father. As we pulled out of the parking structure, I saw her walking out the front door of the building and had the nerve to fucking smile at me. My ears grew hot, and my mouth felt like I was attempting to swallow a cotton ball. I stared at her through the window until she faded from sight. I overheard my dad giving Jay a sort of heads up. *I wanted to say something to my dad. I didn't appreciate him making a deal of it to Jay like it sent me into some sort of clinical depression. I was shocked and mad that's it. Driving me home warning my husband; you'd think I was in the car with my mother.* That fucking smile though it sent me over the edge. "I walked into the house. I saw your husband outside on the porch watching the kids play and you peering on; you looked at me puzzled as I barreled through my front door."

"Do you remember that day?" I asked, not really expecting a response.

The word vomit continues, "I practically attacked my husband, pushed him into the powder room bathroom and kissed him hard. I shoved my tongue in his mouth and tore his pants down replaying the smile over and over again. I don't know why that smile felt like a challenge. Jay was receptive, but kept telling me to be quieter and to calm down if someone might come in." I ignored him. "I took him in my mouth and stared into his minty green eyes begging them to spark a little to grow greener with want like they had so many times before and when they didn't it angered me. I scraped my teeth around the edge of his dick and still nothing. I forced him to sit on the toilet and straddled him. My arms flung as I peeled my top off. I wasn't wearing a bra. I knocked the ceramic vase off the shelf and it shattered beneath our feet. He wanted to stop, I didn't. I rode him ferociously and he said, "B, please," as my tits that aren't as perky as they once were bounced in his face.

I don't say this out loud to Leigh about my tits, they're an insecurity of mine and she doesn't need to know that. But retelling this encounter with my husband reminded me how much I thought he was a fucking idiot in that moment to use our role play name at a time like that. We are having sex and you call me by the name of the woman who just embarrassed me in front of the whole company.

Leigh interjects my thoughts and says, "You don't have to tell me anymore if it's too much." I shake my head and the memory away and say, "Nonsense," before I continue on with the oversharing, "He was close to climaxing. I could tell I picked up a shard of the vase and grazed it down his neck to draw blood and sucked. The crimson stained my lips, I kept sucking his neck as I ground down on him in the most animalistic way. He came in me hard. I felt the gush of warm liquid fill me and I wanted to stay in that position, but as I sat completely content, he grabbed his neck and pulled his hand away to gawk at the red on his fingers. He practically threw me off of him to the ground as he looked at me in such a way. I can't even find the words to describe it. A little disgust met with fear and confusion. What a sight I must've been with my blood-stained red lips smiling up at him. He mumbled, "Christ, Em," under his breath and hurried out of the bathroom. I could hear voices asking him if he was okay. I sat there a spell, ran my fingers over my lips and smeared the blood onto the white wall.

"So you see, unfortunately for my vagina, Jay began to withdraw from me after that, and my father must've told my mom about my breakdown at the office, completely negating the fact that I had a whiskey glass hurled at me by my crazy bitch of a boss which caused my already overbearing mother to lock in on me. So here I am, polishing off bottles of wine from a subscription, avoiding the office and my boss, screening my mother's calls and peering out my window offering you a shoulder and some advice while my own life is in turmoil."

I was rambling through my recount giving her way too many details that she hadn't asked for, even touched on some mommy daddy issues so when I finished and looked up at my neighbor who took a sip from her glass at the same time as I, and was blinking wildly, she simply said, "You're crazy. Maybe we should consider some help," and she laughed so loudly that I began to laugh with her and our laughs in turn became one. Laughter's good for the soul. Laughter is also said to be a natural pain reliever so maybe if our night continues like this, I'll defeat this headache. Laughter, however, is not good for a husband to hear on an accidental butt dial while he thinks you're home alone. She's so fucking soft spoken he probably can't hear her; he's looked at me like I was a basket case since the bathroom incident. Anyway, this couldn't do much more damage. I look at the green connected line on the phone, put my 1-minute finger up to my friend and scurry out of the room.

"Jay." I say, he sighs deeply. "I'm right here, Em."

"I've got the hangover from hell," I say, "but I'm fine." He sighs again. "I miss you, who you were, who we were…"

"I miss you, too," I say, "but you'll be home soon. Work trips are never very long, and I will get us back."

Now I see why Leigh wants to go to Therapy.

He stutters a bit and yet another sigh. I can't quite figure out why he's sighing with such exasperation like he's annoyed and saddened at the same time. "Look," I begin but the line goes dead, my neck jerks back a bit out of surprise. Bastard hung up on me. I stared at my phone as Jay's tone lingered in my mind like a bitter aftertaste, and the weight of his indifference pressed down on my body's fragile state leaving me feeling heavy with ache and regretting my decision to bite the dog that bit me. I head back to my study, but only my wine glass remains. I must've taken longer than I perceived. The contract of time has been a doozy for me today in any regard. I'm alone again in my dimly lit space. Alone with the thoughts that have plagued me all day. Alone with the memories that keep rearing their ugly heads.

"He's on his way back." I whisper aloud. Yes, I love him enough to fight for this. I promised I would. I let my ex slip away too easily. I wouldn't make the same mistakes again. I kiss my favorite picture of him in my home because even though I've declared I'm fighting for this, I still needed to physically acknowledge my heart.

# DO MY EYES OR TIME DECEIVE ME

It's funny the idea of letting someone go. Sure, physically you can do it, it's tangible, it's measurable; you can see and feel it, but mentally emotionally how do you know you've truly let someone go?! My thoughts trail off because I hear him, he's home. My body grows anxious. My heart skips a few beats anticipating being wrapped up in his arms. I am practically sprinting to greet him to let his love wash over me, but my body comes to a complete halt when I hear his voice. My Jay is speaking, but to whom? And about what? I am struggling to catch the sounds echoing off the walls. My first thought is he must be on the phone discussing something or the other regarding work; until I hear, "B," and I know the conversation is about me. I step quietly creeping toward the glow of the living space he's in. His voice is laced with concern. There's a certain sense of vulnerability in each word. Each word that I am beginning to discern as I draw closer to him.

Jay pauses a breath and as he does, I catch myself holding my own breath in fear of what's to come. When Jay finally opens his mouth to speak again he says, "There's a distance in your eyes, I can't place where you are most days. Help me, babe, help me understand are you lost inside of that beautiful mind of yours?" He sucks in a deep breath and shakes his head back and forth as if he's rehearsing and now my heart is racing and I am feeling shameful; my cheeks begin to flush as if I am intruding on a personal moment.

I know I've been distracted, but I didn't realize it was this bad. So bad that my husband can't talk to me. So bad that he has to rehearse his lines before he even kisses me hello after time away. I am wrecking my brain combing through all of our latest interactions trying to pinpoint any moments that may stand out. Does he know my mind drifts to *him* at times, can he sense that? I pause my worried train of thought when I hear Jay continue, "I can help, I know the signs. I too ignored them out of denial and hope, but we are at a crossroads now and something must be done, we cannot continue this way. I cannot continue this way, our family doesn't deserve this."

I creep to angle my line of sight so that I can see more of him in this vulnerable moment. I am teetering on the lines of just going in there and telling him I heard his speech and I'm here ready and open to listen and figure this shit out, but a stab to the heart prevents that. The crimson lips and dark hair of a woman dance into my view and I instantly gag and throw up. Having nowhere to expel the waste I force myself to swallow it back down. It takes herculean effort to not allow the noise associated with my further gags to escape my mouth and draw attention to my presence.

I begin to blink furiously hoping the next blink will make her vanish so that I could blame it on my imagination or the tainted wine. I wanted my eyes to deceive me, but they didn't; each blink made the figure clearer—it was Barbara standing next to my Jay, nodding silently in my home. Looking ever so empathetically at MY husband. The shock and betrayal I felt, is he really standing there rehearsing this intimate moment that should be reserved for me with her of all people?! How did this union even come to be? Did she follow him home, stake out my house and jump when she saw him pull in the drive, or are they having an affair and so bold and brazen to bring it here? I lean closer toward them because I hear that the bitch has begun to speak. I hate her voice, it's brash and sultry and everything she says is a command. For a woman after my husband, she's playing the fence between being a home wrecking whore and having my back? My face is lace with confusion. Barbara is telling him about how she thinks I am fine, and that work is just stressful even with my lessened load. How she is sure I'm worried about the children and it's consuming me and she thinks just a little rest would do me wonders. She doesn't think a therapist or any drugs would do me any good. She said it'll probably make me worse. She teases, "You know her and her silly aversion or phobia to doctors and hospitals. Imagine what forcing her into a situation like that would do." "Hmmm," I say in my head. She's right, the last thing on earth I want to do is see a doctor. Besides that, there's one very obvious fact they are failing to mention. I am fine! There is nothing wrong with me! I am not sure what her play is, but how dare she address my fertility issues to my husband? That's my greatest insecurity, my biggest heartache aside from *him*. Her tone, mannerisms, and her vocabulary while showering my husband with her unsolicited opinions of me are ever on par with her personality. She's so bold in declaring how well she knows me and how she knows what's best for me. I am laughing inside burning with rage because this woman doesn't really know me, not from a can of paint. She only knows what I show her or tell her, not all of me. No, she doesn't have all of me. There's still a tiny morsel she hasn't touched.

Though I can't say the same for my husband she keeps touching him! She presses light touches to his shoulder or hand every time she speaks. I can feel my own fingertips burning blistering with anger and fear. She's laying it on thick telling him that she does mental check-ins with me all of the time. That if she truly thought I was a danger to anyone including myself she would be the first one to tell him. *When the fuck did they get so close?* "Trust me," she says, "this is nothing a little time and love can overcome." She emphasized the word love so much that she made it sound dirty. "I know when someone is crying out for help and I intend to answer those cries, you can count on me for you, too." She ends with a wink and a bump from her hip to his. *Lies. She only shows up when it's most opportune for her.*

She says that ultimately, she understands his concerns and it's a scary path to walk, but she warns he shouldn't be too hasty in his approach. His eyes are locked on her collected demeanor. I can see them trying to ignite but struggling, he looks truly tortured like he's teetering the fence on whether to trust what he knows is right in his gut, or listen to the very convincing ramblings of this woman. I can't help but fixate on the way he looks at her, his eyes shine a fiery green if only just for a moment, the way they used to for me. The way I'd been trying to get them to shine again doing anything I could to draw the fire out of him all this time. She saw it, too. I could tell by the way she crossed her legs and squeezed them together. She lit something in my husband and she was proud of herself not only that she was aroused.

I can only assume Jay began to stride toward our liquor cabinet to break the sexual tension in the room. Jay's gate is slow and hesitant as if he's contemplating something. Once he reaches the other side of the room he steals a glance at Barbara over his shoulder and proceeds to fetch a bottle and 2 glasses. I couldn't quite hear him, but from what I could see the evidence suggests he must've offered her a drink because she acknowledged his offer of a crisp white wine and declined by scrunching up her nose and waving it away. She peeled herself off the stool and walked over to where he was and reached for the decanter of Jameson accidentally spilling the wine. She apologized profusely and slowly bent over to clean the spill. My Jay handed her a dish towel and she knelt beneath him sopping up the liquid. At that moment I urinated on myself. Shame spreading across my face how humiliated I'd be if they saw me here this way, but I can't move and I can't look away the familiar pang of betrayal is stabbing me in the chest. *He* did this and got caught in the rapture of a dark-haired witch. She tricked him, lured him in with promises of freedom, and an endless supply of dick sucking. She was taking advantage of him in his fragile state and he couldn't see it. I loved him and him, me. He thought I didn't know when she snuck in to be with him after her shift. I could smell her on him; I always knew. Now here I am meeting the same fate with a different man. I can't describe the scramble my brain is feeling. It's akin to my accidental sniffing of an alcohol pad as a kid, the sizzling of the brain that doesn't immediately go away, the direct burning feeling that hurts but in an incomprehensible way.

The soft hum of laughter brings me back to the nightmare I'm now reliving, kneeling in a puddle of my own waste, the stench starting to creep up my nose still I am unwilling to move. I watch as Jay smiles down at her and says "careful" in a flirty voice. "Apologies, Mr. James." she replies. Then cocks her head to the side like a puppy waiting for praise or direction. The puddle of wine is still surrounding her.

I am losing my mind silently. I am hyperventilating and a million thoughts are running through my mind starting with the most important. Why do the ones I love so deeply always want to replace me? Barbara and I weren't very different. I mean I modeled myself so well. Barbara and I are almost the same. Why would Jay turn to her? What was I missing and what did I fail to do? My father tried to replace me, granted he was replacing my mother, but I was so much like my mother back then so much of me came from her. If he replaced her, he replaced me in turn. We were never enough. Then *he* tried to replace me. I am plagued by the constant conviction that my love is never enough no matter what I do. They always need more and not from me. They always look elsewhere to get their fill. It's always the same type. It's always everything that I am innately not.

*I swore I got it all right with Jay, we were happy, what did I do wrong?*

*How will I survive this, should I tell my parents? Will they believe me?*

*Why wouldn't they believe you, Em?*

*You know why.*

Jay is a knight in shining armor, a goddamn Prince. I can't go to them and say I am leaving Jay because he fucked Barbara. They would both call me delusional or paranoid. My mom thinks I am too wrapped up in work and turning into some maniac throwing tantrums and obsessing over children. If she gets wind of this and I have no proof, she'll push that agenda again. My dad is so fucking enamored with Barbara I am not even sure he'd hear me out. The beauty and brains that is Barbara, a young enigmatic go-getter he once called her. He'd never quite used those terms to describe me. I suddenly realize what I've said to myself. I cover my mouth at the revelation I am triggered by my dad's relationship with Barbara. It's like losing my dad all over again, there are many similarities between her and Barbara. I laugh that I hadn't noticed them before. This makes perfect sense and this just won't do. It's one thing to try and steal my husband, but it's another to take the first man that ever loved me. The only man that never stopped loving me. First, I'll need tangible proof just in case I need to show them.I need her name tarnished and her holier than thou persona killed in my father's eyes. I set up my phone and swipe to the camera to record and watch with heavy breaths. Double checking my phone is charged and the two snakes before me are centered in the frame. What they're doing right now is innocent enough. Although I don't like it and it's definitely inappropriate, it's not enough to prove anything. I need more. I need Barbara to do what I know she wants to, I am counting on her. *She will deliver as she always does.*

I am caught between a rock and a hard place. I don't want to watch, but I can't bring myself to turn away either. Part of me is pleading that Jay comes to his senses and stops this before he does something he can't take back. I know he won't based on the look in his eyes. So I decided to watch the transgression through the tiny phone screen. I know it sounds ridiculous, but it makes me feel one layer removed and not as pathetic and vulnerable. I hold my breath as I peer on as Barbara grabs Jay's ankles using him as an anchor to scoot her entire body closer to him. She peaks up at him through her lashes and bites down on her lower lip and then she slowly drags herself up the length of Jay's body pressing her body firmly against his growing erection. "Prick!" I mouth to myself at the betrayal or his manhood as I shake my head left to right. A large part of me was holding on to hope that I wouldn't see the bulge in his pants on account of her. That hope was shattered. Once to her feet she swallows the rest of her glass, leans into him so that her tits are sitting just beneath his peck, a perfect bird's eye view for him, and she reaches her arm behind his back and slams the glass down. "Shhh," my cheating bastard husband says, "you'll wake the house." She giggles, fucking giggles like a school girl, stretches up on her tippy toes and licks my husband's lips. What I did not expect was for this diabolical witch to turn in my direction and lock eyes with me. I wasn't sure I saw what I saw. I quickly look up from the screen and I am frozen in shock.

Barbara's gaze is so confident, so cocky as if she'd known I'd been there the entire time as if she was waiting, daring me to stop her knowing I wouldn't. That lick to my husband's lips was her calling me out of hiding, luring me out, daring me to stop her. I feel my mother's spirit taking hold of me and I am furious with the sadness, weakness and pure defeat surrounding me. I worked so hard to build myself up and this is happening again. Did I not prove myself the first time or the second time? As my husband buries his face in her neck, she arches her back and he palms her ass all the while; she never once looks away from me.

I am fixated on Jay for a spell and I am consumed with jealousy. I keep questioning how could he be so comfortable to do this in our home knowing I am here, it doesn't make any sense. Have I been so out of my mind drunk on wine for weeks that he thinks I wouldn't awaken to witness this? How could he touch her like that, how he touches me?! Why does this look so natural like he's done this before, like he knows her body? Knows just where to touch, kiss, lick. I am driving my sanity further and further away with each passing second, but I remind myself this is not his fault. No matter what. It's the ballsy witch's fault. I silently chant it is not his fault over and over.

Barbara has always been ballsy. I guess you have to in order to pull off some of the shit she does. While I am in awe of her grit, at the same time I am utterly embarrassed because I am attracted to her at this moment. The way she came into my space and took over like she belonged hereand I was intruding on her life and not the other way around. I desperately want to sprint as far away from here as possible, her eye contact with me is paralyzing, she's got me strapped into a front row seat of my worst nightmare and as he hikes her skirt up and begins to undo his pants, I watch Barbara making the most intimate eye contact with my husband. She's arching herself on the table and running her fingers down the space between her breasts. I am stuck, sitting in the dark corner of hell that is a part of my house that my body won't move from. I can't stop myself from running my fingers down my stomach trailing slowly, lingering in the most sensitive of places hovering around my own sensitive bulb of nerves. I don't know why, but I am mimicking Barbara's every move yet I am drenched in urine and I feel nauseous at the difference between her and I right now. My body is responding with arousal while my mind is full of shame. I get this sudden intense gut feeling pounding at me causing the floodgates of hatred to open up, releasing me from my trance, and I run as fast and quietly as I can to my study curl up in a ball and pleasure myself to the image of *him* and *her*. Hell I picture all of them. The orgasm that erupted from me felt far better than sitting around and crying ever would. I may have cried if this was my first rodeo, but it isn't, this outcome will be different. The release I so desperately needed provided clarity. I'm going to eliminate Barbara, before she eliminates me. Simple.

At some point I must have dozed off because I feel his hands on me as I'm willing my eyes to stay shut. He's holding me so tenderly repositioning me into our bed as if he didn't just fuck my boss/friend/enemy in my home. The fact that I don't recall falling asleep prods at my already questionable memory. I did just witness my husband commit adultery, didn't I? My days are blurring and so are my thoughts in the most extreme ways.

Deep down it has felt like something bigger than a hangover, something deeper, but I've been reluctant to admit that. My exterior is a stoic sleeping angel, but I'm smiling inside a devilish all-knowing smile. It's not Jay's fault and I forgive him, just like it wasn't *his* fault. Barbara is a threat, threats get eliminated. Jennifer was a threat and she was eliminated. I made the mistake of taking my emotions out on my ex when he was a victim of circumstance. I won't do that again, steer off the usual course of action. This is my husband after all, and I'll do what I need to protect him from this leeching woman. Hell, I needed to protect myself as well because for some sick reason I still admired Barbara. I mean, in my defense, she nurtured me and gave me confidence when I lacked it. In part I owe some of my success to her, a mentor of such she was. But this betrayal is gnawing at me. I wish we could be friends and coexist in the same spaces without her feeling so threatened by me. It's obvious that's what the issue is, when she feels threatened by me, she puts me in my place. I've allowed it but that's over now. She knows I saw her and she thinks I won't do anything about it. She's wrong. She doesn't realize the consequences for this web she's spinning will cost her her very existence. I'm inviting her and my neighbor over for girls' night in, *and I love a good girls' night.*

I'm using my neighbor as a buffer and alibi. Poor thing she doesn't know, but she's meek and mild and I can't tell her the truth she'll fold under pressure I mean look at her, she let her husband leave with her kids and cried about it instead of springing into action. That's not the type of personality you spring a murder plot on and expect her to be ride or die. Because I'm going to kill Barbara like I should've before, but I misdirected that anger, and repeating the same actions and expecting a different outcome is a sign of insanity. That I am not.

# CHAPTER 8

# B&I, THE 1ST GIRLS' NIGHT

Another dance of opening and closing my eyes. Part of me believes I'm the one prolonging the inevitable; the nagging voice in my head confirms it. This tango is exhausting in and of itself and the worst part of it is I'm confused. I'm admitting this reluctantly because I don't remember the last time I felt so lost. It hasn't been this bad in a long while it had to have been High School days, but even then it was never this bad. It hasn't been this bad since I was able to study under Jennifer and Barbara. It has actually never been this bad since I made the decision to be the polar opposite of my mother, but beside all of that I am still confused. Saying it out loud is a no; that would just give some power to my mom's concerns and some valid reasoning as to Jay's pulling away and not to mention just yesterday my neighbor, Leigh, called me crazy.

*Yesterday?* A voice laughs.

*Yes, yesterday. I think.*

She was joking though, right? It was all in fun since we were sharing and drinking. She wasn't actually calling me crazy. I tell myself firmly needing reassurance. I am awake at this point, but I feel like I am in one of those dreams where you think you've awakened in reality but really you're just awake in your dream. Or like you're waking up from a movie of dreams right into another. The only thing that lets me know I am conscious is the fact that I am still partially hungover. Hangover and dreams aside; I saw Jay cheat on me last night. I know what I saw and what I felt. I am stalling getting out of bed so I don't have to face him because I am not sure how my body will react. A full-blown breakdown, punching him in his face, or playing it cool. The latter is what I needed, but I am as unpredictable as the weather. The house is eerily quiet given he is notorious for making the most noise in the morning blending his smoothies and brewing his espresso. Jay is home, isn't he? He'd have no reason to put me to bed and leave. Where would he go? Home with Barbara? I laugh. But instantly stopped because although I wouldn't think there was a possibility in hell for that to happen, after last night I am not entirely secure in that anymore.

I am not secure in anything anymore and the feeling is maddening. I tiptoe around lurking in corners and slowly opening doors only to be greeted by silence and emptiness. So I am home alone. Was that even last night when my husband had his tongue down my boss's throat? Did he leave with her? Did I dream of it? Nodding my head in disbelief has been a second nature motion to me lately needless to say I'm confused. I know I am not making these occurrences up. I know they happened. I am just confused by the timeline; I can't quite place everything. Who can blame me? I've had a hangover for 24 hours straight. I think. Alone with my thoughts used to be a safe space now I am not so sure. I am replaying my conversation with Leigh, am I spiraling, too? How can I be sure? AH! I scream. "Em, you gorgeous genius, you recorded the cheating bastard!" Finally, I will have a date stamp to help me piece together the fragments.

I was just heading to retrieve my golden device when my head panged suddenly, viciously, and to view came empty prescription bottles, an empty bottle of Jameson, and a puddle of red wine. And just as fast as the view came it was gone. I don't know what to make of what is happening to me. I may very well have alcohol poisoning. I need to see a doctor.

*Go ahead and get admitted you'll love that.*

And as quickly as I wanted to run to a hospital and see a medical professional, was as quickly as I decided against it. I won't go to one, but maybe one will come to me? Do doctors still make house calls because my limbs are stiff and I'm still so cold. It's still so dim in here and now I need to lay back down. I am over exerting myself and feeling an anxiety attack looming.

I lay a short while trying to piece together when the fuck I turned back into my mother. Needy and helpless, needing someone else to step in for me. The timeline in my head is spinning, each memory bouncing like a ball in a roulette wheel the date the ballbelongs to? Tuh, your guess is as good as mine. I sigh. I let silence consume me and I sit up in sheer horror and panic. I did it! I exclaimed in a loud whisper. "Girls' night I did it. Fuck!" I scream a loud scream that is so loud it isn't audible. My heart is racing, where is Barbara? Did Jay find her? Is that why he isn't here? Where is Leigh? Did I do it before or after she left? How much does she know? To view comes the tree toppers merlot's shit, when did I do it ? How long have I been hungover? Where is Barbara? Remember, please remember. Your life quite literally depends on it. I'm frantically scrubbing my brain for it to produce some clues from my fractured memory. When I first woke up, I was cold. Did I leave the heat off to prevent a smell? Was I successful? Is Barbara's rigor mortis setting in while she lies in my basement, or is Barbara on her way here with the police to slap me with a warrant for my arrest for attempted murder?

I didn't feel like this before. I didn't panic like this. I don't even recognize myself, why is my mind and body betraying me. I'm confused, my breaths are short, the room is closing in on me and I'm desperate for air, for escape. I hear ringing in my head and my mom's voice is so clear. I look to my side and my phone's connected; when the fuck did I answer? "Honey bee, is that you?" she says and the ringing in my head reminiscent to a heart monitor gets louder and louder and the beeping is so intense, so intrusive growing in speed, continuing rapidly until it flatlines.

****

What an awful sound, the flatline. I've never experienced it in person in an authentic way, but I imagined the sound reverberating through me when I lost my love. I imagined the rushing of feelings and blood and sounds to your brain all at once in an implosive way, and the noise of it all gets so loud in volume and then just stops, leaving nothing. That's how it felt when I lost him; like I, like we, flatlined. I've only felt this way once before when I was younger. It was a day that will forever be etched in my brain. The day my father introduced my mother and I to *her.* I was in college and my father called to invite me to lunch. He said my mother would be joining us and we would keep it near campus so I wouldn't have to travel too far. He said he had news but he didn't elaborate, I would've never guessed she was his news. I was getting along just fine in college, enjoying myself even. I had a single room which was good for me. I needed solitude sometimes to think. Without eyes on me, you know, college dorms are the size of a closet can't so much as sneeze without misting on your roommate. College life is packed with distractions, and as I mentioned, I'm quite high-strung and easily agitated. Coupled with having one of those addictive personalities, I can't envision having a roommate working out well for me. I am well aware that this is alarming, I consider it one of my many character flaws because that's all they are, flaws, and everyone has them. Let my mother tell it, what I had was an illness or a disease and I should be diagnosed and heavily medicated, but it's a good thing I never let her tell it.

I walked into the fancy as hell restaurant and my eyebrows rose a bit. My dad did well for himself so I wasn't too surprised as it isn't upcoming for us to dine in such an establishment, but this place was swankier than usual and it didn't fit the bill for a simple lunch with my mom and I to share some news. My mom stood from her place at the table to kiss me hello. I wiped the sweat that began to glisten my palms as I took my seat. I was growing anxious not knowing what this was about, I hated guesswork and I couldn't stop myself doing it. I needed a distraction so I looked to my mother to ask if she had ordered a beverage while she was waiting. She was beautiful, but she didn't play up her potential which infuriated me. I remember the heavy sigh that escaped me when I first laid eyes on her that afternoon, my very unassuming by all accounts ordinary mother. Why didn't she try a little harder for things that should matter to her, why didn't she try in anything? Her looks, her career, her relationship with my dad, me. Maybe he would've married her if she'd just tried. I took a seat next to her and opened my menu engaging in forced small talk. I was beginning to grow impatient, my legs crossed under the table, but the right one shaking uncontrollably as I bit down on my bottom lip eyeing the menu. I looked up ready to bark at my mom as three figures entered the establishment stealing my attention. I locked in on them and the room spun when I recognized it was my father who had just walked in with a leggy brunette. She sported French-manicured nails and had her hair pulled back into the sleekest of buns, with a mirror-like sheen that seemed almost crystalline. I could swear I saw myself in her hair. The warm glow of the sun that shone through the windows and back lit her as she walked up literally shifted and provided her with the softest spotlight. That same sun that basically turned her into a goddess did nothing for my mother. I wondered if it did anything for me, but for her it highlighted her cheekbones, and made her eyes the warmest chestnut. It accentuated her defined jawline and added just the right amount of sheen to her lips. I almost couldn't stand to make eye contact with her. Her being Jennifer Bailey; better known as "B." B came bouncing up to our table wearing the biggest smile and smelling like heaven and introduced herself to my mother first, then me. She grabbed my left hand with her right hand and covered it with her left, cocooning my hand in hers as she pulled me in to kiss both cheeks and gush over how she has been looking forward to this moment "forever." Forever, I repeated in my head mimicking how she emphasized the word. I glared at my father who was too busy staring at Jennifer's ass to notice. I would've responded to Jennifer with more words. I'm not that rude, but the only words I could form was, "Oh." I was tongue tied at best because I was so stuck on the diamond hanging off her left ring finger.

The announcement of their engagement by my father that afternoon was soul crushing. He said he needed the other two most important women in his life to finally meet the woman he wanted to marry aka "B" that's when it happened. The first time my world flatlined. At a swanky restaurant in the middle of the afternoon. I was so angry for my mother! How dare he and how dare she smile and congratulate them. My mother was sitting here cheering on a man who couldn't marry her, and being positively pleasant while he's introducing her to his fiancée. Vile. If my memory serves me right my parents were just fuck buddies several months ago so him showing up here engaged to the spitting image of businesswoman barbie is comical.

Once the shock wore off mostly for me and we sat back down, I took inventory of the situation. I cracked my neck and smiled matching Jennifer's plastered on red lipped smile all night. When I studied her I could see the appeal. She exuded confidence she was smart as hell, too. I mean not smarter than me obviously, but that's neither here nor there. She was however working in grad school full time which I found to be inspiring. While I was busy studying Jenny from the block, my mother and my father were chatting it up, laughing about old times and discussing how he met Jennifer. Jennifer didn't seem not even the least bit bothered by my parents' familiarity she looked on almost lovingly. At one point she excused herself to the bathroom claiming the drinks had caught up to her and once she was out of earshot, I did the same and trailed behind claiming I had to go too, but quite frankly I was intrigued by her and I didn't want to let her out of my sight. She didn't use the restroom, she just went in, took a deep breath, fixed her face which was perfect and needed no touch ups and strolled back out. She lied, which I didn't like, that was her first mistake. The bartender grabbed her attention and asked if she'd like to sample the menu's new cocktail. She eagerly skirted over, grabbed the glass and took the sample shot straight back. She winked at the bartender and said, "Perfect," on her way back to the table. Her second mistake. I found myself uncomfortably close to her, as if drawn by some magnetic force. She caught my eye, fully aware that I had witnessed her shameless flirting with the handsome young man. In response, she winked at me as she passed, exuding an air of royalty, before returning to her seat and kissing my father. "Touché, bitch, touché." The bartender noticed the disapproving grimace on my face and then asked me if I wanted to try his little concoction. I rolled my eyes at him, I am no one's second choice, he should've asked me first. Back at the table, Jennifer Bailey sat looking exquisite, each movement deliberate as if she came from a realm untouched by the ordinary. In the short time it took for this woman to walk into the establishment, share a meal, and depart, let's say three hours, I had concluded—Jennifer Bailey and I could not exist in the same realm. "B" would pale in comparison to me, in comparison to Barbara. She was the blueprint. Was.

****

The night of the First Girls' Night came after my father had been begging me for months to give "B" a chance; He proclaimed he loved her and he needed me to love her, too. "It would mean so much to me, honey bee. You won't be able to truly know her if you are never around her." Fine. He was right about that. I didn't know enough about her and I couldn't formulate a plan without intel. I needed her gone; like I said only one of us could exist and she wouldn't go away if I didn't send her away. *If only my mother would've gotten my father to marry her, I wouldn't have to go through this. If she loved him like she was supposed to.*

I was finally in the right headspace to deal with my problem head on. I was just going to start by laying the groundwork. I asked B if she'd like to get drinks in the city with me and maybe a bite to eat; she responded before I could even suggest a date and time with an, "Absolutely meet @ the fan at 7." I responded with an, "Ok." I didn't like how she commanded the conversation like that, she hijacked my invite and made me feel like I was the prey.

I did ultimately go to the fan though everything in me wanted to decline and suggest a new date and time. I can't describe it, the feeling of not wanting her to win.

I didn't have a plan for tonight, tonight wasn't supposed to be the night, but when an opportunity presents itself you take it. I was feeling extra confident these days, my darker tresses and my new makeup and workout routine had given me that little extra spark I was missing. I had Jenny to thank for that. She hated that name, and insisted I call her "B." I called her Jenny anyway. When I arrived, she was waving me down from her seat at the bar. She had placed her jacket on the back of the stool next to her to save my spot. She kissed both cheeks as she had before and flagged down yet another googly eyes bartender to take our order. Jenny ordered merlot and a caprese appetizer. I ordered a cranberry vodka with a splash of club soda and extra lime. She smirked at me after my order and it made me feel small in comparison to her. It was then that I knew she fucked up, but she was blissfully unaware.

I quickly shot a text to Jenny saying, "I am so sorry. I have an exam and I really need to attend this study group, but let's reschedule for tomorrow." I text her that at 7:09 p.m. when we were sitting next to each other. I saw her get the notification and when she read it her eyebrows scrunched and she smiled at me waving her phone in my face questioningly. She said, "What's this about?" I shook my head and laughed softly as I leaned in and playfully tapped her thigh before I said, "I didn't mean to send that. I actually thought it hadn't gone through must've been delayed.I was going to cancel on you, but I figured we probably needed this night and there would be another study group early tomorrow morning." So I came anyway. She nudged my shoulder and winked in approval. *What is up with her and this winking shit.*

I convinced "B" that she had to stop being such a granny and we should head a few blocks down to the happening bar and do some shots and dance. She would've done just about anything to win me over. I could tell by the sincerity and longing for acceptance in her eyes. So we did exactly as I suggested.

The toxicology report said alcohol poisoning. My dad was beside himself inconsolable when he called me to deliver the news. *They say if you pass away from alcohol poisoning your pulse becomes erratic, your breath shallow, your vital organs stop functioning, it's a silent painful death, a lonely, really humbling death I am sure.* I hailed a cab because they were harder to trace back than uber and lyft. I could pay cash and not have an app tracking payments and locations. The driver was young and attractive enough so I knew I could do what needed to be done. He almost didn't let me throw her lifeless body in the backseat because he didn't want to be caught up in any shit; those were his exact words. I let my hair down, licked my newly painted red lips and leaned into him and said, "I just need to get my drunk friend home. She needs to sleep it off. My phone is dead so I can't call an uber and you're like the only actual taxi I've seen tonight." I exclaimed breathless and pouty. I climbed up front with him and he drove. At this point I was trying to plan my great escape because I had provided him with a random address about 25 minutes away so time was of the essence and his pestering was blocking my critical thinking. I almost didn't have to do it, but he kept calling out for her and getting no response. So naturally I did what anyone would do in my position. I ran my hand up his thigh, leaned in and licked his neck... His expression was pure gold. Bulged eyes, an instant smile and quickened breath. He was probably 40, definitely married, he had a plain gold band hugging his ring finger and obviously his morals were not completely intact which would play into my plan nicely. His wife wouldn't like this; I mouthed the words, "Sorry, hun, c'est la vie." And I began. "Pull over into the parking garage on the left, put the car in park and don't say a word." He looked at me a bit confused but he obliged. Once the car was in park I continued. He went to turn around to look at Jennifer, but I pulled his face to mine and touched our noses and whispered, "Shhh, as much as I wouldn't mind an audience she wouldn't be a very fun one in her current condition. Let her rest." Which was a very true statement since she was dead. "Do not fucking move, look straight ahead." And then I licked his lips. I pulled down my stockings and placed his hand in between my legs. I dipped his finger inside my warmth and licked it off, he was a puddle naturally. I said, "Unlock the doors and take it out. I'm coming around." What a pure fucking idiot so caught up in getting his rocks off he didn't realize I did not need to get out to climb on top of his pathetic dick but I digress. I grabbed my clutch discreetly, got out of the car slowly seductively to keep up appearances and b-lined it through the garage. I left him there, gobsmacked and blue balled and quite literally up shit creek to figure out what to do with Jenny, no trace of me.

# CHAPTER 9

# THE JENNIFER B EFFECT

For the sake of my good conscience, *what's left of it anyway* and my father, I was going to give her a chance. I had every intention of giving her a chance if it weren't for my mother; *mostly*. I couldn't erase the look of sheer heartbreak in my mother's eyes that day at the restaurant. I knew it was heartbreak because my eyes read the same when my mother looked at me; I saw mine staring back at me, in the glassy sheen hers portrayed... I didn't love my mother's personality flaws, mostly I hated them, but something in me wouldn't allow her to suffer in silence again like she had so many times in the past. I had an irrational fear of being replaced. I could see my mother shared in that fear. The moment she met her she knew she was finally being replaced, her time was up. I couldn't bear to witness it. I wouldn't let it come to fruition.

It started innocently enough. My intention was to spook her

off, maybe be too much of a daughter, you know the kind… needy, spoiled, two faced; enough to make a woman want to run at high speed in the opposite direction. I blame Jennifer for being the deceitful woman she was because of her I didn't even have to get into character and turn myself into a nasty brat, because Jennifer was gracious enough to show me that not only was she not her true self with my dad, but she had ulterior motives. She already had 2 strikes against her from our very first encounter so her sloppiness allowed me to so easily learn of her ulterior motives she literally dug her own grave. So a simple scaring off wouldn't suffice the crime since I now knew she was after more. Like I said, my father is pretty well off, having his successful company and all, she'd be able to upkeep this posh exterior of hers becoming his Mrs. for sure. Unfortunately for her, she didn't foresee me and I wouldn't allow that to happen.

*"Your intention was never innocent, nothing innocent comes from stalking someone."*

I'm beginning to hate the voice of reason that intrudes my thoughts. She is often loud and, in my opinion, wrong. I've been practicing being more direct, putting more intent behind my actions and not allowing outside influences to sway me so as of late she's been getting quieter, I enjoyed that. I wondered what more I could do that would keep her quiet. I closed my eyes envisioning how much anguish I would resolve within if she was no longer a strong voice, just a lingering presence to check my moral compass from time to time, something easily forgettable and dismissible. I am not certain how to do that. I think that would require me to not have a sound conscious at all.

I work in silence. I internalize most things so while developing my plan I spent most of my days lurking in the shadows of my beloved Jenny, I scoff at the thought. Though sometimes she did surprise me with her genuine actions and the little voice in my head would tell me to reconsider, like the times I watched as she walked into the quaint coffee shop that she enjoyed patronizing more often than not. It was just minutes away from my father's office building, a short walk. When she was at the shop she sat there for hours on end and read most often or listened to audiobooks. Maybe it was music, I couldn't be sure. She'd be jotting down notes, grabbing parfaits or the newest pastry item on the menu. Chatting up the barista, making silly faces at the toddlers with their parents and petting every single fluff butt dog that moseyed in with its owner. This was a hard pill for me to swallow because nothing about her seemed quaint when we had been in each other's presence. Everything she showed me was commanding and domineering and yet here she was. Normal pleasant, quite lovely actually. I would enjoy this, this is right up my alley, sitting here chatting, sipping a latte, sharing makeup tips with each other. This is unfortunate, I made a mental note to come here. Just because I can't come with Jennifer doesn't mean I can't come at all and I tucked it away right along with all of the positive sentiments I was feeling toward her. I didn't need a reason to like her, I needed every reason not to.

Jenny was fit, I mean everything on her was tight: her ass, her tits, and there was no sag in her arms. She wasn't that much older than me, but I'll admit she was in far better shape and that was a bit infuriating. I shouldn't have been surprised at the hell like torture trailing her in and out of gyms would be. I wasn't fat by any means, but I shared my mother's shape, pear-like ass and thick thighs. I didn't mind the ass, but my thighs could use some slimming and my stomach had just a bit of pudge, but thanks to my withdrawal from my classes this semester…

*This was a pressing matter that required all of my attention so do not guilt me.*

I now had the time to dedicate to my research. I was up at 4 a.m. on a treadmill a few rows from Jennifer Monday-Thursday. On Sundays she did spin in the dark which was great. It allowed me to slide into the back row and most often the bike right behind hers. No one looks directly behind them in this small ass room full of loud music and other sweaty people at the ass crack of dawn, you go in, do your thing and get out of this 30 min tough as fuck spin class. I almost died in that class panting like a 600lb man, but thankfully my will power to watch her was stronger than my screaming body to give up and it got me through. I watched her in the shower from the crevice of the stained wooden barriers the gym spa installed. The shower nooks were made of frosted glass and wood they claimed was stained bamboo. Her silhouette through the glass was magnificent, but the view from the crevice that wasn't blurred was amazing. I watched how she touched herself, how she was so meticulous and delicate with herself. I mimicked her motions in my own shower down to the very manner in which she rinsed her hair. I reveled in how she used her coconut scented perfume fresh out of the shower when her body was still full of water droplets. I made note of how she put a dab of cream in her hair and a few pumps of a sheen called "glass" and pulled it back into a tight ponytail. She was a little careless in the amount of time she went in between dying her hair. I didn't like that. I could tell she was a natural blonde and it made her look cheap. Her finishing touch was always a red lip, it was like her signature, the shade varied of course but never the hue. Red was certainly her color, now granted it wouldn't look as good with the blonde which is probably why she dyed it in the first place. Her one flaw really did bother me, she should really be more careful to keep up with concealing her true self. There's so many layers in a person's identity the slightest slip up could make it all unravel and her roots were showing. Gawking at me. Confirming how much of a facade she really was.

*She's a liar.*

Most nights when she wasn't encroaching on my father's space she was curled up on her couch watching reality TV with her sister, both of them with longing in their eyes. But Jennifer's gaze was pathetic, practically willing herself to be someone's desperate housewife. Another flaw of hers. It seemed she lived with her sister. I couldn't tell who was older or younger. They looked similar, but not enough to be twins unless they were fraternal. I was guessing and I hated that which only bothered me more about Jennifer not being forthcoming with this sort of information. Her sister also dyed her hair dark from her natural blonde roots, but I couldn't gather much about her even if I wanted to because she was often gone for long spans of time. She was in healthcare and that's all I knew. I didn't care enough to do more research into her. She wore scrubs and was a poor man's version of Jennifer. Not much to tell.

*Disgusting, really both of them pretending to be women they're not.*

Jennifer wasn't a complete gold digger. She worked in a cute office and was involved in law in one aspect or the other, probably a paralegal or maybe even an attorney. I am not sure; I couldn't exactly get fully inside her office without bringing unwanted attention to myself. And because I was so put off by the idea of her initially, I didn't ask my parents any details about her. Plus, the timing would be bad. I hadn't given this woman the time of day and to all of a sudden start prodding like I was interested to learn about her would raise suspicion. The building was a law office though so my assumptions wouldn't be too far off. The office was all glass with a lobby and cafe. The cafe space was a saving grace, I sat there most days and watched as she commanded the hallways with all eyes on her. I was always unassuming dressed in typical corporate office clones attire rifling through manila folders, keeping my head down and sipping coffee. But I watched above the papers in my folder, straining my ears and drowning out other thoughts to add her voice to my lip reading. I was taking her all in. She always wore heels and she spoke with such conviction. I couldn't hear her, but I could tell by her body language. She mostly dealt with men. Not at all surprising she was a slut after all. But I did appreciate how the men lost their train of thought when she spoke and tripped over themselves when she walked by. She probably didn't even have to be good at whatever it was she did; she just had to look good. Mental note made.

At night, not all of the nights after all, she was engaged to be married so she had to dedicate some time to the old man. But any other free night she had, Jennifer spent it sleeping with a young man. He was a blue-collar man. I infer this from the many stains on the majority of his clothing and the rough appearance of his hands. He had a jagged worn look to him that was both sexy and intimidating. I imagined what those rough, large hands might feel like on the delicate folds of her body. He was around very often.

Even when Jennifer wasn't home, he would come and go as he pleased from her place. He meant more to her than just a booty call because he saw the light of day and was super friendly with her sister as well. The three of them were always playfully nudging each other, sharing a snack, laughing at the same mindless show on the TV. I contemplated if there was some incestuous bullshit going on with this triangle, but there was no proof to confirm that.

On a night Jenny wasn't with my father, and the other half of the tweedle dee dumb sister was working the night shift, the ladies made the mistake of leaving their apartment door unlocked. What a beautifully fateful night it was for me. Jenny was moving things into my father's place all day, probably another reason why she wasn't concerned with the locks since she had been in and out so often. This also meant her room and belongings were strung about, she wouldn't bat an eye enough to notice if anything was out of place not that I would be so careless. When I crept into their apartment that night, I took a quick look into her sister's room for any sign that the male was hers and not Jennifer's, but came up short like I knew I would. I made my way into Jennifer's room pausing at the entrance to take in the scent that was so very her as soon as you hit the threshold. I inhaled deeply and smiled. It was a divine scent. I touched little odds and ends as I circled her room. It was white the comforter throw pillows, walls, even the accent rugs were white except for the little hits of red. They were subtle but they made noise! A red flower pot with a sprawling elephant ear plant was in a corner. An abstract painting of naked bodies clung to the wall in varying shades of reds and a candle with red wax. That was it. I moved further into her room and was deep into Jennifer's closet, my new body fitting her clothes like they were made for me. I tried on a few pieces, a top, a dress and began prancing in front of the mirror in her red bottom heels effortlessly. "Thank you, spin class." I mouth to myself as I catch a glimpse of my high and tight bare ass in the mirror. I was full on drooling over myself. I was practically unrecognizable. I looked nothing like my mother at this moment, standing before her full-length mirror with her faux olive tree branches dancing across my reflection. I put on one of her divinely smelling pieces of lingerie inhaling the scent. She must've just had this on, I thought to myself, when a chorus of laughter and commotion came crashing through the front door rudely interrupting my fixation. I hastily grabbed my rags off of the floor and scurried into her closet burying myself behind boxes of shoes and a few coats, leaving the door open as it had been when I arrived.

I took a few deep breaths to slow my heart in preparation for my slower breaths to come. I watched as this cheating slut ripped my father's heart to shreds in front of me. He would never know, I would never tell him, but I felt it for him. I internalized it all. I didn't see her in the act, but I heard her. She spent several minutes in her living room laughing with the young man about a video they had just watched on the phone. Her voice grew closer as she was entering her room. The man changed the subject and expressed his concern for her sister's safety. He mentioned her working nights at that type of place worried him. I rose an eyebrow there because what type of place was he referring to and why would he care so much about her sister's safety if he was fucking Jennifer? Unless he's over using the gentleman card. Jennifer said her sister was a big girl and she could handle herself plus there was security. The boisterous conversations about absolutely nothing went on for what seemed like eternity leaving me cramping in my confined hiding space until finally, the bedroom lights were turned off. It was pitch black minus the light from her phone.

There was silence and then Jennifer opened her mouth and she began to speak so directly, filthy and intoxicatingly. I didn't hear her man friend say a word. He was likely in more shock and awe than I was crouched in the confines of the closet salivating. *Wow.* I panted. I honed in, not wanting to miss a single syllable she said.

Jennifer directed, "I want you to lay down on the bed and close your eyes. Imagine me walking slowly toward you, savor that moment, that painstaking moment where you want me to walk faster, but I simply won't. While you lay there, I want you to take your shirt off and expose your chest and hard nipples, but leave your pants on. I want the bulge straining against the jeans you had on. I want it growing so hard it hurts when it presses against the jeans, but you get no relief because I said so. I want you to know you're not going to cum tonight; you're going to beg me and I am not going to allow it. You're going to save it for me while you listen to me pleasure myself here and moan in your ear."

I practically came myself; I couldn't believe the assertion of dominance. How did she do that? Command a man in such a way that he didn't as much as utter a sound, obediently following her every instruction. I listened to Jennifer pleasure herself right next to a man, showing him she didn't need him at all. If I didn't hate her, I'd want to salute her and ask her to take me under her wing. I found myself saddened for a split second. The least I could do was take mental notes for later. I imagined she touched herself just as delicately as she did in the gym shower. I noted everything about her tone and the words she used. I repeated the words over and over in my head until I drifted to sleep.

The poke of an unruly hanger jolted me to consciousness and I woke up in a slight panic cursing myself for falling asleep. That was a very risky mistake. I crawled out of my hiding place sloppily putting my clothes on. It was 3 a.m. Jennifer was asleep, but she wouldn't be for much longer and I tiptoed toward the front door never removing the red bottom heels. She wouldn't need them for much longer and they were practically made for me. The man was asleep on the couch. I found this odd. "B, what you doing, crazy head?" he said, playfully rubbing his eyes. Luckily, my back was toward him and my hair was now the same shade of chocolate brunette as "B's" I simply waved him off. "Yeah, okay," he said in a sleepy voice, "don't get into trouble. I am tired of bailing you two out." I let out a playful sigh and waved goodbye with my back still turned to him.I heard him settle back down and change position on the couch. With the door closed behind me I raced down the fire escape stairwell. My heart practically beat out of my chest. I didn't stop running until I hit the crisp early morning air. Jennifer would be up any minute to hit the gym. I hope the man is sound asleep when she prances out of her bedroom so that he doesn't have the opportunity to question where she was headed not too long ago. But I wouldn't be attending the gym today. I was exhausted and reeling with memories of what I listened to last night. I wanted to practice and apply it. I wanted to reenact it. I needed to learn more, but time was of the essence I needed to plot Jennifer's dismissal more than anything.

When I got home, I put B's shoes up in a box at the top of my own closet for safe keeping. I kissed the box before I left them there. I didn't get any decent rest last night so my first plan of action was a nap. I laid down and tried to fall asleep, but the nagging voice in my head wouldn't let go of Jennifer's boy toy, it kept questioning the man and his casual tone. *Who was that man? Wouldn't he be in bed too if they had sex last night?*

****

Over the next several weeks I sat through quite a few torturous dinners with my father. Dinners I used to enjoy where I was the center of discussion. Discussions where he praised me for all of my hard work and gushed about how proud he was of me. Now the only conversations my father and I have are centered around wedding planning, her, and me spending time with her. These were several annoying hurtful weeks of my father pestering me about this god forsaking woman. "Come on, Em, just see a movie, grab a bite, maybe drinks. I just need you to try." I almost felt bad, but he did this to himself. It was one thing to replace my mother, but another to replace me. The fact that he hasn't been the same towards me since her was all the proof I needed. And besides, he had no idea that she was sleeping around on him, in essence I was doing him a favor.

*"Replace you? No one is trying to replace you. I thought this was about your mother!"*

I'd had enough, I'd given my dad a chance to get rid of her when I sent him to her place with flowers to do a pop up, suggesting, *"It would be sooooo sweet, women loveeeee this sort of thing."* I had reason to send him there. The blue-collar man was at her house and I needed her to be caught in the act. This was the warning my father needed to take, but he was so oblivious and so dumbfounded and bewitched by this dark-haired siren that when he arrives he shakes the man's hand and hugs him as if they're familiar. Jennifer does have a brother. I learned this at dinner one night. My dad mentioned the brother wasn't from around here and was just getting on his feet after a tough breakup and Jennifer was invested in making Atlanta shine so her brother would fall in love with the city and stay, but I'd never met him. I'd know if this was him though and this man looked nothing like the brunette sisters so I dismissed the thought.

*You don't know anything. You should know better than to judge something based solely on its surface level.*

I was left with no choice, and this was quite unfortunate because the more I learned about her, the more I liked her. We just couldn't exist in the same world, her and I. I knew I needed to open the lines of communication between myself and B so I initiated a string of texts where I'd ask her her opinion on make-up, salons, the best place to get a facial, etc. This was pivotal information and it served a dual purpose. I needed to build a better rapport so she'd be comfortable meeting me for drinks. I truly did want her opinion on those things. Like I said, I admired her. We talked about men, school, my dad which tasted like vile in my mouth I stayed a consistent pleasant step daughter to B and at the right time I sent the invitation to girls' night text to my Jennifer and the rest was history.

# CHAPTER 10

# ADMITTED

I must admit I didn't think it would take my dad soooo long to get over his fiancée. I get that he had proposed to her and planned on marrying her so naturally he would mourn what he thought he was losing a little, but in the grand scheme of things he hardly knew her. He knew Mom and he knew me best. He should be focusing on what he still has which is us, and he's not. In fact, he barely speaks to us. Mom and I have to go to his house to drag him out of bed to make sure he is eating and showering. He doesn't answer my calls and texts regularly and if he does, he is very short with me. My mother says he hasn't been to the office in three weeks. She is worried for him; she wants to make him an appointment to see someone to work through his grief. She wants to water down my father, medicate him and turn him into her, she's got some sort of sick obsession with mental health professionals. They brainwashed her during her stint in the gray

I Am convinced of it, but I won't allow it. He is just a little heartbroken. We've all had a breakup that rocked us harder than the others. I will get him through it. The thought of him seeing a therapist and talking to them while he is barely speaking to me is making my blood boil. I can't help but think if he would be this crushed if it were me lying dead instead of his precious Jennifer? Shouldn't I matter more, shouldn't he love me more? Hard to say at this point. Needless to say I am feeling disappointed that he's still grieving. Grieving what? I don't know and I don't understand; he didn't even know the real Jennifer, not like I did. I knew the ins and outs of her. I think I may have spent more time with her in those weeks than he did, I knew her intimately he barely scratched the surface. I loved her too, but you don't see me barely existing. In fact, I am having the opposite experience. A lot of me is beginning to awaken thanks to Jennifer. I owe her one.

Two months had passed since her untimely tragic death and my father's grief had turned from tortured heart alone wallowing in his sadness, to a hound dog Pitbull mix. He was relentless with the detective assigned to Jennifer's case. He would press them for what leads they were following and accuse them of doing piss poor detective work. He was at the precinct weekly delivering any new bit of information he could think of any tiny morsel that came to his brain, he was there. He was hell bent on getting the detectives to start working this case as a homicide, because he does not believe she died from alcohol poisoning and a drug induced overdose. My father was adamant that Jennifer would never do drugs; she cared far too much about her mind and body. Jennifer's siblings also gave statements similar to my father's in that regard. "She would never, she had never," blah blah blah. They were all right as annoying as it is to still be pining over this woman all these months later. I know what they said to be true myself based on her dedication to the gym and the contents of her fridge and medicine cabinets.

My father had even gone so far as to conduct his own investigations. He stopped at telling people he was a detective because he wasn't dumb enough to land himself in jail for impersonating an officer of the law. But like I said, he turned into a Pitbull. The bartender from the first place was likely close to filing harassment charges. The poor guy has told my father time and time again the same story that never faltered from the statement he gave to the police; that Jennifer left with a female friend who resembled her. That was all the young man knew. He pulled copies of her receipts that gave a vague time frame of reference and clearly showed she wasn't drinking alone, but really, it was a dead end. Though because of the description of the woman Jennifer was with, most people assumed she was with her sister; despite her sister insisting she wasn't there. I even suggested she was probably with her sister to my dad for shits and giggles. I do know her sister was even regarded as a suspect for a period of time. But one way or the other she was able to provide an alibi that checked out and they took her off the list of subjects.

For myself there was the matter of my text messages found in her phone. Even though it said I canceled that wasn't enough proof. I had been called in for questioning. My father insisted I have a lawyer present so I obliged, but played calm and collected because I had nothing to hide. At least that's how I needed to appear to the detectives. I told them that I had every intention of meeting up with my soon to be step mom that night and I sobbed and said how I should've just gone and maybe this wouldn't have happened. I cried a little harder and whispered just loudly enough in the interrogation room, "This is my fault!" The detective and my lawyer rubbed my back, I was brought some water and I was finally able to gain composure enough to continue my statement. I was rolling my eyes inside. I said I had been struggling a little in classes so much so that I even withdrew, I was so ashamed of that I had been hiding it from my parents, but the new semester was right around the corner and I really needed to study. Sometimes, my undiagnosed ADHD was a huge detriment and there was a practice exam so I needed the extra help when it was around. I claimed to have been in my room all night, unfortunately alone. I prayed to the Almighty that my story was enough and they wouldn't or couldn't check cell phone locations from where a text was sent. The police did subpoena my school for the dorm's hall security footage on my floor. In addition, they asked my RA to come in and give a statement; he stated he did not see me exit or re-enter my dorm that night.

*Of course he did.*

I was cleared with no further questioning.

My dad was the one to report Jennifer as a missing person when he hadn't heard from her in over a day. Of course, the police didn't do anything for forty-eight hours. My dad was on pins and needles, her siblings were none the wiser, they assumed she was just shacked up with my father busy with working and turning my father's home, *MY home,* into hers. When my father got the call several days after he had reported her missing, he sobbed uncontrollably into the phone. I had the misfortune of being with him at the office. He was notified that her lifeless body was found by a homeless man in an alley, this was a pretty famous alley known for scoring drugs. The homeless man who frequented the spot told police he had never seen her around there before, and he only got authorities because he was hoping she might still be alive and he wouldn't be able to sleep if he could've saved her and just ignored her. *Noble guy.* The homeless guy who the police wanted to question further must've gotten out of dodge, he may have been a homeless druggie but he was smart enough to know they'd try to connect him in some way so he was gone. I laughed at the thought. My father refused to believe she was an addict, but unfortunately her toxicology reports proved otherwise. He said someone must've spiked her drink. He was absolutely shattered but honestly, I've had enough. Two months was long enough. He wasn't the same doting father he once was and that just wouldn't do. I had to do something to get his attention, to drag him back to me, so I did what I had to do and threw a bit of a tantrum as I like to call them out of love and cue my ever-growing distaste for hospitals. Reluctantly, I was admitted.

The doctors called my flare for the dramatics by way of my perfectly thrown tantrum a manic episode. They hinted at depression and a few other things I chose to ignore. They suggested I do inpatient therapy. The suggestion is just their way of making it seem like there was some choice to the matter. They admitted me as a danger to myself. The suggestion goes one of two ways; voluntary or involuntary, but either way you're going. I knew this, but I channeled my distaste for not being the center of my father's world for him inviting another woman in, and I told myself there was nothing I could do about it. I tried my hardest not to allow the voice of reason to come through she had been trying so hard lately, and then told myself to silence her like I had with Jennifer, apparently that looked like so:

An unknown man dials 911 to report blood curdling screaming and loud banging from an off-campus dormitory. The police broke the door down I can only assume due to me being unresponsive. I winced a little at the thought because I know my father will have to foot the bill to replace the door. According to the police report, when they found me, I had smudged red lipstick strewn about my mouth, and was completely nude with the exception of the red bottom heels. The ones I "borrowed." My hair was slightly damp, the reason for that I don't remember and I had a few bruises on display from throwing myself against the walls. The state of my place was chaotic and a little creepy I may have gone a bit overboard; I had shattered wine bottles all over the floor and the walls were covered in red lipstick markings it just looked like scribbles at first glance, but known only to me they were in fact the letter "B" in cursive in both capital and lowercase letters I thought it to be poetic. Beside my limp body were sleeping pills. I didn't drink all of the wine. I am not an idiot. I wasn't actually trying to off myself. I had a few sips from one glass and took 4 sleeping pills, then made myself vomit around 20 minutes later for safe measure; I needed to feel it, but I wasn't about to kill myself, I was just getting started.

I have the tendency to go to extreme lengths to make the chips fall how I want them to, or at least consider the extreme, but when the steel gray door clanged shut and the stench of sterility burned my nose, I instantly regretted this. I made a very strong protest once I had to remove all of my jewelry and anything with loose strings or sharp points that I did not belong here, that this was a mistake. I was panicking so much I even yelled that I did it on purpose and pleaded not to lock me away, my protest however fell on deaf ears. I was immediately seen by a nurse who took vitals and carted off to a psychiatrist, who had a brief 30-minute intake conversation with me, read the police report and dismissed me. I was then escorted to my room given water and a nice handful of pills that the nurse checks your mouth for after to ensure you've taken them and left to my own devices. The initial process is so cold and so lonely. I laid there on my hard mattress and scratchy blanket curled into the fetal position. If I had to admit this, I was afraid and overcome with regret until an unsuspecting wave of tiredness came and swept me away.

The first several days in the gray I was removed. I didn't talk to anyone but my therapist. I followed the schedule, ate the garbage food and stuck to myself. The voice of reason was so loud in the initial days that I was riddled with guilt and disgust for myself. How had I let it come to this? I couldn't just be happy for my father suck it up and live with the fact that I would need to share my father's attention. I don't even know how much true weight my mom's heart really held; sure I cared, but I didn't kill Jennifer for my mother so she could have a chance again. Admitting that to myself tasted so sour in my mouth. I killed someone, I drugged a woman and ended her life and left her like she was nothing. I teetered on the line of coming clean, admitting everything to my psychiatrist and living with the consequence I deserved. The problem was staring at the ends of my hair where the chocolate brown still shone, when I stared at my hair it would quiet the sound conscience trying to take over.

The hideous fluorescent lights flickered above me. I knew this lighting was doing nothing for my complexion. I sigh resigned to the fact that I would be sleeping here for the foreseeable future and I'd be subjected to the gray. I am starting to feel more like myself. I mastered letting the pills sit just at the nape of my throat enough to where the nurse couldn't tell I had not swallowed them fully and I could easily cough them back up. I hated those pills. They turned off everything in me that made me, me. I was more vibrant these days. I had studied the successful patients to a T. I knew exactly how I needed to behave and what I needed to say to get myself out of this hell. I happily participated in everything even though inside I was dying with disgust.

Group therapy was the worst of all. All of these sad, lifeless people moping around acknowledging themselves with such diseases based on what I would call a fairly normal reaction to some unprecedented occurrences. That's the problem nowadays. No one can be passionate about anything, if you're too passionate you're crazy or overbearing. It's ridiculous.

*You're one of them.*

The staff in all of these places just sit up on their high horses, their expressions impassive, and impatient ushering people to and from. Looking down on the clientele as if they were any better. They're all one bad day away from ending up here too whether they wanted to admit it or not. The entire place had no warmth, no small talk, no talk of love, dreams, desires, inspiration, nothing until...

Group was held in a large, wide room with small windows at the far end. Just as stark gray as everything else, the room contained a door that haunts me daily. The door, the darkest shade of gray, was heavy and cold to the touch. It teased freedom, yet when closed, it seemed to smother the light out of your very being. The click of the lock reverberated, internally it felt like it sealed my fate within these cold confines. I let the weakness in me take over for just a moment in times like this where my thoughts have no fire behind them. In these moments my mother has won and I am where she believes I should've been so long ago.

My mother whom I love is not as innocent as she seems she's always been envious of me. She said I replaced her with my dad. It's why she wanted me here. I'll keep this golden nugget of revelation to myself. I won't hurt my mother, she's a victim of her own sad mind.

I had a role to play and I would do it seamlessly. A familiar faced woman with a voice that annoyed the living hell out of me, whom I never bothered to get to know, spoke often in group. The poor thing was really trying especially in the beginning, she got here when I did, She told stories like,

"I hear voices that others don't. It's like there's a constant conversation going on in my head, commenting on everything I do."

"I sometimes believe things that others find irrational. Like, someone being out to get me or take something that belongs to me or replace me."

"My thoughts get jumbled up, and it's hard to organize them. It's like there's a chaotic storm in my mind, and I struggle to make sense of things."

"There are times when I question what's real. It's like there's a blur between what's in my mind and what's actually happening around me."

I can't stand to sit next to this woman when she spews this shit. I don't make eye contact with her; it's like she's speaking to me, willing me to agree with her. I pray to God she's not contagious. She doesn't attempt to talk to me any other time; she's just there looking at me, watching me like a creep. I've caught her staring at me at the most inopportune times like when I swapped my anti psych meds after accidentally bumping into the nurse and causing her to drop something, Or when I creep out of the staff break room and Rob appears several seconds later and heads in the opposite direction of me. One time I even thought she tried to address me.

*Please stop, pull it together and take the meds, we were so close to breakthrough.*

I heard come from a faint voice whose pitch sounded a lot like hers; but she wasn't facing me and the voice was so soft and she just continued walking right past me without so much as a glance my way. That was smart of her, I was a bad enemy to make and I am not sure I would be the righteous friend she seems to need at this juncture. On top of that, I really didn't have the bandwidth to deal with her too. I had enough on my plate and something else heavily on my mind.

I'm so thankful for what walked in reminding me of life itself because I was heavily medicated for the first half of my stay. I was not my charismatic multifaceted self during most of my time in the gray. In the desolate confines of these walls, I was losing touch with myself. The medication they forced down my throat had an unwelcome companion named silence. I felt quite empty. I was uncomfortable. I don't do well when I am uncomfortable. I internalize things I've said before and I wasn't able to do that under the influence of the meds. I was just empty. It was the sacrifice I made to get my father's attention back. But it wasn't a sacrifice I was willing to withstand for long. Mastering the throat trick literally saved my life.

My father visited 3 times a week and with each visit he boasted about how proud he was of me, and how he couldn't wait till we could put all of this behind us, and I just knew that included Jennifer, and that was the glimmer of hope I needed to push through. On that visit my dad triggered a memory of Jennifer and I clung to her and the ends of my hair for dear life. Jennifer lit a fire in me through that visit. I knew I could count on my dad and love to bring me back. Afterall, love is all we need.

Love is indeed the most important thing to me. I harbored a love that defied conventional norms and my love manifested in unpredictable ways. I knew this. When I loved something, I felt a magnetic pull to them. I would study them, watch from the shadows, eyes gleaming with fervor, with love. Where things tend to get a little sticky for me is how I act on that love, it's intertwined with devotion and possessiveness. I would call it passion, though.

When you do things passionately and give it your all, and those things are rooted in love, then the universe will see to you. Hence, I am happy to report my sacrifice was indeed not in vain. I almost forgot Jennifer myself, but the medication when some did seep into me was very sobering and my dad was a very strong reminder as well. My subconscious wouldn't let me forget what I did no matter what. I however just had to remind myself what the root of my actions were and that I am so thankful for the impression Jennifer left on me and I was able to get through my days fairly seamlessly. However, I did feel a bit stressed when I was affected by the miniscule amounts of medication because I couldn't quite figure out why I did it, I couldn't make sense of it. I had no rhyme or reason that truly made sense. I wasn't jealous. I had always had my father's attention. I'd never feel threatened and my mother barely loved me. Why would I protect her heart in such a way? But I know myself and I don't just do things I am meticulous so I just knew in my core she deserved it.

Aside from my father's profound visit, the next best thing to happen to me before I almost lost myself completely was to befriend the lead security guard; Rob was a middle-aged recovering alcoholic who still indulged but only on the job ironically enough so he could sober up before heading home to his placid wife.

Obviously, Rob didn't make the best choices while under the influence and that gave me the upper hand. Rob spilled all about his wife, he went on and on about how she didn't appreciate him, how she belittled him and never treated him like the man he was. Rob was an athlete who played in the minors and sustained an injury. He wasn't THAT good so the injury put the nail in the coffin of his mediocre career. The wife was only with him for the money she thought he'd make and so when she fell pregnant, she kept the baby to secure her financial footing and now she resents him and the kid and doesn't give him any. Yes, I sat through nights of a whining partially intoxicated man spilling his heart out just so I could use it against him at a future date if need be.

The ace I always had in my back pocket that I did not lose in this hell hole was my blessed genes and the fact that I had adopted Jennifer's workout routine and stuck to it even after her passing.

May she rest in peace, my muse. So my body was still just as it should be. I, in short, fucked Rob into next week every chance I got, he was putty in my hands so ultimately he did whatever I asked of him even when that meant swapping my pills for placebos and getting me the good shit when I needed it. He never questioned why I asked for whatever was on my list. Good sex causes men to lose brain cells, I guess. He even smuggled me hair dye and cosmetics. Rob was my saving grace until some nosey nurse reported him for inappropriate conduct. It seems Rob had been very handsy and flirtatious with said nurse. Men, you can't trust them as far as you can throw them. I am almost offended that Rob wasn't faithful to me, but he served his purpose. My luck had not run out as I had been granted release from the gray hello color!

Hello color, hello you.

I was late to the group, the day I really saw him for the first time. I saw glimpses of him before, but it was just a glimpse and he never emerged. I had graduated from this hell hole, but I volunteered and often led a group which they loved because of my success story. I did it for one reason; *him*. I never told my love why I was late. I didn't want to hurt him, but I needed things at the time. Things I didn't have access to as a former let's call it attendee and I had to keep Rob happy as well so what they didn't know wouldn't hurt them. The hospital failed to collect Rob's badge upon his great exodus and I needed that badge to access all doors, especially *his.*

# TAKE IT

I graduated from the psych ward with my parents by my side cheering me on, fresh out of the bin. The looney bin that is. My dad, just shy of being good as new from his fiancée's untimely death, was dapper as ever fitted jeans, an oxford shoe, a plain white button up shirt, and a tweed blazer freshly cut hair, and a trimmed gray beard. A handsome guy if I must say so myself. My mom wore a frock of a dress that was 2 sizes too big, her hair pulled back into a loose braid, a pink tinted lip balm and just a touch of mascara looking as homely as ever and putting a foul taste in my mouth.

*You'd think after what you sacrificed for her she'd get it together, but of course not.*

The thought that came to my mind felt like acid on my brain. I felt pure utter disappointment in my mother. My mind wandered on the car ride to the restaurant for my celebratory dinner, and the disappointment I felt towards my mother settled like a heavy fog. My mother's life was a monotonous routine of work, wine, and whining about my father... As my mother, when I needed her most she was absent, or passed out on the couch wallowing in her own self-hatred. My mother was clinically depressed. She doesn't know I know. In HS I found all of her prescriptions, all of her writing journals where she admitted not knowing how to love me and love herself, how she only valued herself worthy when my father valued her. One passage noted how after having me she felt less valued by father, like she only served as an incubator to bring him what he would love forever and she was just discarded. Her battle with depression made me resent her. She replaced my happy childhood and teenage years with a subdued existence that left me yearning for more of everything. I was lonely and bored. *She never noticed, lost in the mundane that is her.*

My mom had potential, though. When she was medicated and putting effort into herself there was a shimmer of spark in her eyes, but it never lasted. Depression is an ugly beast. I learned all the tell-tale signs that she was about to crash the hard way. I spent a lot of time internalizing everything and studying her. I only started having issues in High School with my attention span and having healthy boundaries because she let me sit and simmer alone in a pool of resentment that silently grew into pity and a longing to get her to wake the fuck up. I developed an immense passion to be nothing like her, to be bold, pursue my dreams, never let anyone walk over me and live a life full of color and warmth and love. I was going to love ferociously with every fiber in my being.I find it nauseating that a mother didn't know how to love. It took me absolutely nothing to love B. I knew the woman I wanted to be and since my mother wasn't a good representative of that woman, I had to find her and create her on my own.

The car ride was monumental for me. Sure I had already been acting on this, but I solidified it in my mind that evening and that made all the difference. I was going to be "B" the kind of woman who could get a catch like my father and have him crawling at her feet and begging to marry her. I was going to have a life of color. I've always loved the color red. I was never brave enough to embrace it. It was too much for me and my pale skin and auburn hair. It would overpower me, it would wash me out. Not anymore with my rich brown tresses the color wrapped around me like a warm embrace, shielding me from the cold colorless reality that I lived through, that I was never going to return to. Red can evoke a myriad of feelings and emotions. The strongest and most profound are often love and passion. Yet, there's also an association with darker elements like murder and blood, which I don't particularly relate to. Red is also the color of his hair, his full head of hair that I couldn't wait to run my fingers through. *I was going to have him.*

Dinner was presented beautifully and the flavor set my taste buds on fire, since I had been eating cardboard and air for several weeks. I ordered the surf and turf with a cabernet and my mother ordered the chicken and vegetable medley with a pinot grigio, typical. My father had stuffed salmon over a risotto and he paired it with the cabernet as well. I was cutting into my medium cooked steak participating in conversation in between bites. I was actually enjoying both of their company, it was quite pleasant until my mother decided to pay me a backhanded compliment on my looks. The tone was so questioning it made the hair on my neck stand up.

"Well, honey bee, you did it, I couldn't be prouder. I was a little nervous with what happened, but it all worked out in the end, didn't it? Next up your graduation." I nod. That was a loaded statement. "But honey bee, this look of yours is very bold. I miss your light hair, you looked like my little mini me..."

*Exactly.*

"And the red lipstick, wow. It's quite the choice. Taking make-up lessons, watching those YouTube videos or something? Or did you get inspiration from uhm maybe someone?" My brows furrowed and I twisted my mouth in annoyance. I didn't mean to let her see that she had ruffled my feathers, but it slipped out. "Thank you, I think." I swallowed my steak and placed my knife down with the point in her direction. Not purposefully it just panned out that way. I raised one eyebrow and with a smirk I said, "Definitely direct inspiration, but I had it in me all along I just didn't know."

"Had it in you?"

"Yes, Mom, the balls, to embrace new things to be who I was destined to be, to erase who I am not." My dad, the clueless man he is in this moment raises his glass and says, "Cheers to soon to be college graduates with the balls to change their look and own it!"

"Cheers!" I say as I wink at my mom. She doesn't smile at me or wink back. She actually dips her head down just slightly and says cheers a bit lower than everyone else and swallows hard. I think she might be afraid of me. That's ironic, it's almost poetic how the tables have turned. I was afraid of her all those years and her incapacity to love me.

The drive home felt endless, my mother's demeanor had changed now that I was in the backseat and she was up front with my father. Partaking in chit chat and laughter, her and my father nudging each other sharing inside jokes. I rolled my eyes behind them. They must be fucking again and she must be steadily on her anti-depressants. Pathetic. Toxic combination for her she doesn't learn her lesson ever it seems. If she wants him, she needs to just say it, she needs to just take him. Put her foot down already. If she thinks I am going to prevent her from being replaced again she's got another thing coming. I can't put myself at risk anymore for her to squander away the opening I provided for her. As much as I do for her, I wonder if she feels any love toward me at all now. She's been clingy and needy, but that's a direct result of not having my father's attention. I don't remember the last time she said I love you. Finally, the car comes to a stop. I can exit this sexual tension fueled vehicle. I kiss my parents goodnight and head into my building. The relief I felt back in my apartment was immense. I couldn't wait to be alone to get back to what has been on my mind for weeks now. *Him.* My volunteer days have been spent watching from afar. I didn't want to scare him off and I wanted to find out his quirks, his likes and dislikes so when I went in for the kill I'd have the upper hand. I spent my nights at his bedside as often as I could.

We made love not too long ago. It was tantric, it was beautiful. I sat in the cream leather recliner that was angled next to his bed. I whispered nothing but affirmations in his ear. I told him how much I loved him, how strong and brave he was and how I was so proud of him. I sat pantiless in the cream chair and took my heavy sleeping man's hand and placed it gently over my bare vagina. I closed my eyes and gently ground into his hand envisioning his mouth on mine and how warm his body would feel on top of me. My breaths were ragged and short. I was practically panting under his touch. I could imagine him tasting of peppermint and a hint of whiskey. I could hear the rasp in his voice telling me how perfect I was and how he loved being buried deep inside of me and that's all I needed to gain release. Thankful for that divine timing as I heard the jingling of keys in the short distance outside his door, so I quickly pulled my leggings up and left my juices saturating his hand. He loved that I did that, I could tell we had an unspoken thing between us where we just knew what the other needed. I ducked under the frame of the metal bed. I couldn't risk us getting caught. He'd be heartbroken if he couldn't see me until he was released. Heavy footsteps approached and a bead of sweat rolled down my forehead stinging my eye. I watched the shadows under the slit of the door, but from where I was under the bed I couldn't see to the glass windowpane to tell who was about to enter.

I could tell by the shadow that cast on the floor and the scent that wafted in that a woman entered my James' room. She had long stringy dark hair that draped down to her calf as she sat on the bed and leaned over to take her shoes and socks off. I was confused as to why any nurse would be doing this. I heard him groan and shift in the bed as if he was moving over to make space for her and then her voice pierced through, "Eww what'd you do jack off and fall asleep." A low deep giggle returned her question and then silence. I fell asleep on the cold linoleum floor and because I was so careless, I didn't see or hear her or him leave. I wasn't sure what to make of that interaction. The possibilities were burning a hole through my heart and because I don't like to guess I chose to file it away.

*You chose denial.*

Having to lead a group and get through my senior capstone was taking up a lot of my spare time. I also had to focus on landing a job post grad because I wasn't going back to my mother's place. On top of not wanting to go back there I had to keep up appearances. I was thriving and that kept my father happy and my mother off of my back. I was at my local watering hole polishing off my second glass of cabernet laptop propped up, when she walked up to me and said, "You remind me of myself before, keep going you'll be exactly who you want to be." I thought I saw a ghost and I'd be willing to bet my freedom on my face being the shade of freshly bleached bed sheets and if it wasn't then lock me up and throw away the key. The woman standing before me was immaculate. About five foot 7 and clearly in shape though she had a bit of hip making her shape a bit more womanly than B's. She had her hair in a low bun that was slicked back and she was a milk chocolate brunette. It was hauntingly like looking at Jennifer with just a few subtle differences. I shook off the instant intimidation I felt by this gorgeous woman and held out my hand and said "Thank you, I know, my name is Em, and yours?" She nodded and smiled and repeated the fact that I said, "I know," and replied with, "Barbara, and I think you're someone I want to know, my dear. I am joining you."

"Please do." I replied and flagged the waiter. "Whiskey neat," she said as I closed my laptop.

After last night I am not sure who I love more, Barbara or Jameson. We had so much in common as we ordered small plates and glass after glass of wine I told her all about Jame and I and how I was graduating from college in two short weeks. I left out how I had already celebrated one graduation this year. She told me to drop by her office at the end of the month with a resume and she would see if there were any openings even if it was just a paid internship. I was grateful for the offer, but I was also infatuated with her and her uncanny resemblance to B. Barbara was a brunette who had more legs than torso, a solid full B cup and she was probably a size 4, high and tight round ass and another one for the slick back look except hers donned a part on the side it looked so good on her. Last night I repeatedly had to chastise myself after I had caught myself staring at her too hard and for too long. But I swear she was a sight to behold, that woman looks like she steps out of the bed in a fully pressed tight as skin skirt and stilettos. Her skin is pristine and I would kill for it. She just might be Jennifer Bailey reincarnated. A long-lost cousin maybe because Oh My God.

Barbara told me she didn't do relationships because one person never loved as hard as the other and someone would always be short changed. "Relationships are more trouble than they're worth." she said. "Get a dildo or a fuck buddy, it will be less headache in the end." But since I had raved about how in love Jameson and I were, Barbara gave me a tip to keep things moving with him since I told her the physical part of our relationship was slower than I'd like. I am not even sure how she got me to open up so quickly about my personal life, she may have missed her calling as a therapist; one minute we are exchanging pleasantries the next she's telling me to, "Just take it," in reference to my slow-moving sex life with my love. I couldn't believe my ears because I had thought that exact thought about my mom wanting my dad so badly. Why I wasn't following my own advice was beyond me so I planned on using it this week. After all, if you really want something you don't stop for anyone or anything until you get it.

Sneaking in and out of the facility was like second nature to me now. Jame and I played it coy during my volunteer days, we knew the risk that came with getting caught held consequences we couldn't face so we made small talk (I spoke he listened), exchanged pleasantries (I smiled he stared into the abyss), played board games (I moved his pieces for him), and parted ways. But tonight, tonight would be the night I solidified everything for us. I swiped what was now my security badge and tiptoed into the corridor that led to his room. I waited till the 3:15 a.m. rounds were over and made my way to his door. I found him just as I assumed I would. Sleeping like a baby. The past several times I've come at night I wore scrubs. I needed to blend in seamlessly just in case I had got the timing wrong. I also needed something easy on and easy off. Jameson's soft breaths and warm breath made me smile when I leaned over his face to kiss his lips and tie my scrub top around his eyes. He started to stir, but I kissed his cheek and put my pointer finger to his lips and whispered, "Shh." His body stilled and a small smile grew on his face. I made sure to straighten my hair and wear it down. So if anyone walked by, they'd think I was just the nurse from the other night.

*That's not why, Em.*

This moral compass can be really fucking annoying. I waved off the intruder like I had grown so accustomed to doing and slipped out of my scrub bottoms. I tiptoed to the small window in Jameson's door and after one last peek through the window down the long dim hallway, I tugged away at Jameson's boxer briefs and when his perfectly tanned dick sprang free I was salivating. It had the perfect curvature and the juiciest veins. I put him in my mouth and he wasted no time pumping furiously in and out. The gagging noise that escaped me seemed to turn him on and he'd just pumped harder and harder. I grabbed his balls firmly and he held the back of my head still as he plunged in and out of my mouth. My eyes were watering from sheer pleasure and he exploded. He immediately reached to untie his eyes, but I grabbed his hand and kissed him and said, "Tsk, tsk." If he thought we were done he was mistaken. I hovered my vagina on top of his face letting my lips touch his and then pulling up and repeating it over and over until he grew frustrated and hard again and grabbed my hips slamming my vagina to his mouth. I was so close to cumming and I would have if I didn't need to have him inside of me. I dragged myself down the length of his body with my back toward him and rode him; he let low moans escape and it drove me wild to hear him; to actually hear his voice so much so that I exploded all over him. "Hey," he said as he began to untie my top from his eyes. I snatched it from him quickly, never turning around and scurried out of the room down the hall to the staff bathroom and pulled myself together. I didn't want to ruin the night we became one by talking. I wanted to leave him in awe of me. I wanted him to crave me.

The four-letter word haunted my sleep, it followed me to the bathroom in the middle of the morning. It brewed coffee with me and it showered with me. It clung to me for hours and days on end. It wanted to embed itself into my being, flooding me with anger and guilt and grief. What I did was not that. Jameson and I are in love and his body rewarded me by spilling out his pure pleasure.

*He didn't know.*

*He knew!*

*Your world is colored by a touch of delusion…*

*My world is colored red.*

# CHAPTER 12

# HIM

He is reserved for my innermost thoughts, my innermost feelings, I wouldn't share him with the world, I would do him no justice, no one would understand or appreciate or love him like I did. He is reserved for me and my memories and that's where he will stay until my dying day.

I carried on through my days in the best manner I knew; my thoughts always rushed back to him. I was back in the swing of things in school, on track to graduate and applying to jobs. I was modelesque. No one would have guessed of my stint in the gray. As much as I hated it there, I couldn't stay away because he was there. I don't refer to that place for what it is. I believe it could be so much more. Half of these people aren't crazy, just passionate about one thing or the other. The annoying auburn-haired woman whose voice I can still hear from time to time, I swear I see her in passing even though I know that can't be. I know she wasn't crazy; she was smart and articulate, I believe she was just passionate about having rational conversations with herself. Every single person walking this earth talks to themselves. She just wanted to know how to continue to do that without letting the voices she didn't agree with consume her. Meds take that away. I watched her transition. I had a front row seat. The medications just made her void of personality, they made her unassuming and meek, they made that poor young woman my mother. She was aged, but not like fine wine because of the gray. The gray aged her spirit; it wasn't as vibrant as it once was. It's a shame I thought she had so much potential inside.

I still volunteered once a week in a group setting at the hospital. I was making my presence known and being a very positive helpful asset to the nursing and clinical staff. My report card would be full of gold stars if we had one; but where I really thrived was in the hushed corridors of the ward at night. This was the time I gave into my wants and desires and nurtured our love. This was my time to breathe his air, to study him, to engulf myself in his aura. I could hardly handle the time I wasn't there waiting on bated breath riddled with anticipation. I knew he felt the same the way he locked eyes with me during his group sessions. Words were unspoken, but his eyes especially were windows to the soul.

When I looked at him trapped in here underneath the mask of these drugs, I could see that his soul was crying for release and I was determined to free him from the mundane they were forcing upon him. When he first arrived, he came blaring through the door's voice projecting like a siren. He fought feverishly for himself, but he lost the battle. I mourn for him when I see him now. I sit by his bedside and gently stroke his cheek and kiss his lips. During the day I feed him and sneak extra applesauces to him. I do what I can to let him know I see him and he is not alone, where it's easy to just fall in line and blend into the walls. I didn't want that for him. He didn't deserve this, I found myself hating whoever was responsible for putting him here. I know him and he wouldn't have come on his own accord not the way he fought back so hard only to succumb.

Tonight I didn't have time to visit him. The night nurse was away from the nurses' station and I needed to make copies of his file. I was gutted at the mere thought of him waiting for me, looking for me only to not show up. I never wanted him to feel like I didn't love him, but I needed to do this. I swiped Rob's badge that still worked seamlessly. *What a place, huh?*

I was ninja stealth, I knew the exact placement of all the cameras and maneuvered around them so that my face would not show even if pieces of my body were captured in the frame. The night nurse I saw most often wore a bun and had a similar enough physique to mine and chocolate brown hair so the grainy outdated camera system wouldn't highlight any alarming differences.

I planned to get what I needed from Jameson's file on a night where I'd be on the schedule to lead an evening group so that I could see what color and type of scrubs the night nurse was wearing that evening and come back matching her perfectly. It was really too easy which made me feel even worse that my love was stuck in the confines of this mediocre establishment. Should we have faith in an establishment where an average person can so easily gain entry and manipulate things? Absolutely not! I knew time was of the essence, but I couldn't help myself; I creeped toward the hallway that passed his room so that I could at least blow him a kiss through the window in his door before I sped out of sight. That's when I saw her hovering over him. The want radiated off of her it was so strong it pierced through the cold thick metal door. It sent my senses a blaze. She must've felt me watching her. I ducked hastily below the room's window and hauled ass down the hall toward the exit. I paused only to look down the hall toward his room once I was safely tucked away outside the exit door. She was looking back and forth down the hallway for me, or the ghost she thought she just saw. Psychiatric hospitals have the tendency to give people the creeps and make them overly paranoid. The ones who reside there know the only things to be afraid of were the people pushing the pill carts.

I waited until I thought the coast was clear and made my way to the station to take photos of the contents of Jameson's file. I had to pry my feet step by step and endure a gut punch of agonizing pain the further away I got from his room and out of the facility. I wanted to go to his room and haul that slut out by her hair. I needed to know what she was doing in there with him. It was eating me alive that she was breathing his air and I was home alone in my bed without him. My only solace was the file I now had. I sat up on my bed and turned on the lamp and opened my camera roll and I devoured his file. I read every single note, twice.

His parents had him committed against his will. He had an episode in which he accused his brother of trying to kill a young woman named Sarah. Sarah was noted as a woman who he believed to be his girlfriend. According to his file she was an RN and was an active participant in his plan of care and a longtime friend of the family. It was unclear whether or not she was actually his girlfriend. He was so convinced this betrayal occurred he threatened his brother's life, and when confronted with proof that his brother was out of town on business and in fact not here in Atlanta with Sarah, and that she was still alive and well, my poor love accused his brother of teleporting and Sarah being cloned. Upon his brother's return to Atlanta, Jameson broke into his home and hid. Then, unexpectedly, he attacked his brother with a knife. Realizing what he had done he turned the knife on himself and slit his wrists in the middle of his brother's living room. *My love,* I sigh hugging the sheets of paper.

Jameson was transferred to the Psychiatric hospital post his hospital stay to stabilize and treat his self-inflicted wounds.

The therapist notes say that Jameson admitted to not taking his meds for several weeks leading up to the episode. He had pleaded with his parents for outpatient services and vowed not to stop taking his medicines again. Apparently, he had even offered to move back in with his parents so that he could be under their supervision. His parents would hear nothing of it and had him committed.

Jameson was to do ninety days in the gray only to be transferred to another facility for recovery afterward. The second facility was more of a boarding house. There was a lot of structure, but you could leave on day passes and work a limited amount of hours per week.

My heart broke for him reading all of the details, I imagine how it must have felt to be discarded that way. Nothing in this file turned me off. If anything, I was even more captivated by my desolate love. His name was Jameson Anthony James, a man whose haunted eyes carried the weight of unseen burdens. Of betrayal by those who were supposed to love him the hardest, the ones who were supposed to love him through this blip of a moment. Jameson was a strong name. It held a bite the man belonging to this name would not lose himself, not on my watch,

I would not allow it. I will love him through the lunacy. I will love him as they should've. We already have a connection forged in the crucible of vulnerability and betrayal. Our love is destined to blossom.

Now that I knew him even better, every day without him proved to be debilitating for me. I could only think of him. I raced to the facility on the days I led the group and I raced there every other night to sneak in and watch him sleep or just lay beside him. During the days I was volunteering I'd show up early just to sit next to him by the window in the recreation room. He had been here for four weeks and was nonverbal. He just sat there hunched over a sad shell of the man that burst through these doors a month ago. I sat with him though as often as I could I would be here daily, but that would be too suspicious. I would tell him of our love, how I've always existed, he just didn't know it was me. *I didn't know it was me until I saw him.* I told him of our plans for the future little by little. His once oblivious gaze was coming as he was seeing me, he was hearing me, he was smiling. I pressed my lips to his more often than not stealing these moments when no one was looking. I'd wheel him to his room to rest where I'd tuck him to bed after tucking his dick into my mouth repeatedly, he moaned and stared longingly into my eyes until he came. I couldn't wait to get him out of here. I was planning on approaching his parents, cursing them for the trauma they inflicted on my man. I would be corroborating his story telling them I was indeed Sarah, and that the Sarah they knew of was merely a case of mistaken identity caused by all of the medications they were forcing into him. I'd say that I, the true Sarah, had every intention of marrying him and I would be taking over his plan of care. It was coming together so perfectly until it wasn't. Until week six.

Over the course of the last several weeks I had been swapping out his anti-psych meds with placebos as often as I could, but obviously it wasn't often enough. On week six he began to emerge; a profound resilience radiated through him that sparked that all too familiar warmth within me. My heart leapt when he shared in group for the first time. I just knew the man that I first saw was about to make his return, but instead I was greeted by a different version of this man. Jameson opened his mouth slowly and smiled as he apologized to the group for his lack of interest. He said he needed time to adjust and to come to grips with the reality of his condition. He said he needed the solitude to process and make amends with himself. He said he had been having extra sessions with the in-house therapists and that it was really helping. He had embraced reading about his condition and that he'd like to consider today his first day in group and then he began, "Hi, my name is James..."

*Wow, who is this man? What have they done to him? If I believed in clones, I'd say he was one.*

*What the fuck is he playing at? This doesn't sound anything like him?*

*He's smart, he's telling them what they want to hear, that's gotta be it.*

*No, that's not what this is. This sounds like acceptance.*

*No, this sounds like insanity!*

I am paralyzed by the confusion his group share stirred up and as the days pass my confusion stays. The voices in my head are ever conflicting and to add insult to injury my love, Jameson grows distant. His distance is felt by the hugs he gives me that are superficial and cold. The smiles he shines my way are bleak; they are smiles that don't reach his eyes. He's formal with me and doesn't melt into my touch when I reach for him. I think this is my fault, I've made him insecure. I haven't been sneaking in as often at night because I had just graduated and began working at Ingenuity Recovery and it was taking up more of my time than I anticipated, but there was never a moment my thoughts weren't with him. *He had to know this.*

I was new at work though and I had to make my mark. My boss was a force and I had to show her I was, too. She had to know I was everything she was and more. But this was odd and though he and I never formally discussed our future, we knew. It was an unspoken vow—he was mine and I was his whoever he needed me to be. When he'd moaned, "Sarah," as I was swallowing him whole one night I paid no mind to it he knew who I was.

I had to see him to talk to him away from the watchful eyes so I came back over the following weeks with Rob's badge and creeped toward his room. But to no avail things had changed and so had rotation times I had to learn all new schedules. *I didn't have time for this shit.* It was infuriating.

Week eleven is when I caught him with her, the same her, the same dark-haired siren that was hovering over his bed all those nights ago. She was reading something to him, or maybe she was just clutching the papers in her hand as a clutch. Whatever it was that was coming out of her mouth and falling onto his ears was causing some emotion. Emotions I couldn't read from this side of the glass. The close proximity between them and the way she held his hand had my eyes burning holes through the side of her face. If looks could kill she'd be dead where she stood.

I heard the voice of the male nurse on duty and dipped off into the break room and waited ages for him to pass. I decided to check the staff on duty logs, because I needed a name to associate with the siren trying to dig her claws into my man. A name would give me a starting point. *That's all I needed.* To my surprise, there was never a female nurse on at night. I flipped all the way back a few weeks and again it was always males, so who the fuck was this wench?

This dark-haired mystery woman spent most of the night with

him. It was nearly 3 a.m. before I could get into his room. When I opened the door with annoyance clearly written all over my face, he looked shocked and then amused, and cooly said, "Hey, Em," he continued, "what are you doing here so early? I know I am crazy," he laughed lightly, "but it's not your group therapy day?" I tilt my head to the side and brush my hair back behind my ear before I ask him, "What's going on?" He looks utterly confused. I ask again, "What's going on? Who is the woman that's been here all night? This isn't the first time, Jameson." I added with a little extra annoyance to my tone. His eyes grow lighter as if he was relieved and ready to admit defeat, an energy I didn't quite like. He says, "Oh you caught me," almost jokingly. "That's Sarah. She works at the adjacent hospital as an RN. She comes here after hours because of her residency schedule, she can't get here during business hours. It's harmless and I'd appreciate it if you kept this little secret." I was shell shocked; I spit directly into his face and whispered through tight lips, "I thought you loved me." My head panged and throbbed.

*You've done it again.*

*I've done nothing but love!*

Jameson interrupts my internal argument while simultaneously wiping my saliva off of his cheek by saying, "Em, are you okay? Should I call for someone?" I curse him and say, "Why are you doing this? I am your Sarah, we are in love!"

Jameson jerks his head back in disbelief. "Em, we barely speak; I only see you once a week in group. I am out of here soon, I don't know what kind of game you're playing, but please don't drag me into it." I shrug because I too don't have time for games, if he wanted to get my attention for not being here as often he's got it. "Jameson, end things with her now and we can forget this ever happened. I will forgive you, I knew I smelled her stench on you. I should've guessed she'd try to replace me." Jameson grabs my shoulders and firmly says, "Em, I have no idea what you are talking about, I am not ending things with Sarah, whatever she is to me is none of your concern." I am distracted by the warmth of his fingers penetrating my skin, I lean into his chest and lick his lips he recoils. I stare at him with disgust and betrayal before I turn to leave. But before I do, I say with venom, "She's nothing to you." He genuinely looks concerned and says, "She's not anymore, not how I thought she was, but Em, neither are you." The feeling of being stabbed in the back radiated down to my bones as I left his room. He would come to his senses and do the right thing, and if he didn't then I would leave him no choice, eventually he'd see things my way.

I was late to work that next morning. It was one of the roughest nights I had had in a while. There was no calming voice, only anger. I didn't make it a habit to make friends because I didn't feel any of them were on my caliber. I had friends before, before I became what I was meant to be, but they were extensions of a lesser me and I wasn't bringing them into my new chapter. But I did have someone, someone who I valued, someone whose opinion actually meant something to me so the next morning when I got to the office I went into Barbara's office and vented. I told Barbara about my breakup being the reason I was late, she said she had a feeling something was off because I shared the same sentiments as her in regard to the importance of time. Barbara didn't know it then, but she said something to me that really resonated. She said, "Good, end it with him and good riddance, look past him, look right past him and you'll see your true destiny." So I did exactly that. Exactly that! Though, losing him caused me great anguish.

*You cannot lose something that was never really there.*

*You cannot lose something you never possessed.*

# CHAPTER 13

# DAY OF RECKONING

I've given it some thought and while I am extremely annoyed with Jameson, I can't help but feel that maybe he is testing me, maybe this place is testing us. Medicines change people. They're chemicals, poisons really meant to alter your brain's natural chemistry. The Jameson I love wouldn't hurt me like this, and I am hurt, I mean I am soul crushed that whoever he is right now used me the way he did just to toss me to the side like yesterday's news. I was a placeholder for him for his Sarah. A placeholder until she came along just as my mother was a placeholder for my father. But Jameson and Sarah, they are not in love and true love will always prevail, the universe has a way of making things right. I know this because I will ensure it, just as I did before. You can't help who you love you're not supposed to.

The problem that I have to face when situations like this arise is that I am so tightly wound so I can't just let things simmer, there would be entirely too much unbearable anxiety flooding through me to just wait and think on something and then act. No, I act accordingly and think it through as it plays out, there is no rationale, I need instant gratification for my feelings. I am tired of waiting and I am ticked that now I've developed yet another trigger and it has simultaneously been set off because of him and her. I am tired of being triggered and having to fix it myself, I am tired of being replaced by mediocrity. My mother was a 5/10 at best when she remembered I existed back then and then they went and fed her medicines and replaced the only mother I knew with some even keeled mild woman who wouldn't scream if you set her on fire. She didn't scream when I had breakdowns, she didn't cry when I cried, she didn't hurt when I hurt, she barely spoke, she just wanted me neutralized like her. Brainwashed and adhering to whatever they say she should be.

This awful woman is one of them, this woman with her stringy long black hair, her dark circles, crow's feet, 3-week-old manicure and unworldly natural beauty with no makeup. I am studying this woman who pales in comparison to me, the me I am now, the me that would make Jennifer B give me a standing ovation. This woman is bland, nothing about her excites me; her face without makeup does however make me tick a bit because I can see some appeal there and I don't want to. This woman is the worst type of woman, colorless. She fits right in with the gray she should really stay here, an orderly could easily confuse her with a resident if the right circumstance presented itself. I digress.

*Ha, you're truly sick.*

::Cracks neck::

I smile to myself because it would be a feat, but if anyone could pull it off it would be me. Picture me planting drugs on her, digitally altering videos of her acting strangely on the job, cue an inappropriate relationship with a resident. It's poetic and I feel very fond of poetry. It would land her in here or even better in jail. Far away from my love. I can't do that, though. I don't have the bandwidth at the moment and this is about him. If I could just get through to him the real him, inside, buried under the poison I could save him before she and this place kill him. I glance back at the unimpressive poorly shaped woman a few feet in front of me and I can't figure it out. What does the Jameson curated in the gray see in her? Even a man whose brain is laced with poison couldn't possibly find interest in her. Whatever the appeal is I'll find out and I'll do it better.

My ass is starting to numb and I am thirsty. My water bottle is empty and I didn't bring backups because I didn't intend for her to take this long. An asinine nurse she must be indeed, I agree with the voice in my head. I am squinting to see as clearly as possible through the mirrored windows; she looks as if she's charting now, but she's painfully slow. I'm tired of sitting here waiting for her to get in the damn car. I can't see her at the nurses' station for about 25 minutes. My mind runs wild with thoughts of her walking the adjoining bridge to the psych ward and bombarding her way into Jameson's room and proceeding to take advantage of him in his fragile state. I tap my freshly polished navy nails on the steering wheel and then twist my back stretching left to right. I can be patient for things that matter if I were watching Jameson. I could see here for forty-eight hours straight, but this woman is nothing to me, a thorn in my side toilet paper stuck on my shoe and I want this chapter that she's in to be over with now.

I'd pull the fire alarm if it meant getting her out sooner, but it wouldn't guarantee her not going back in and I wasn't going to risk that. Another sixty-four minutes pass before she's exiting the facility. I don't like her for obvious reasons, but there's something else about her that's sounding alarms in my head. Unfortunately for me, my headspace is crowded and I can't quite pinpoint it. I watch as she climbs into her jeep and pulls out of the parking lot. I follow her making sure to stay 2 cars behind to a gas station where she buys a bottle of the cheapest moscato and a pint of ice cream and beef jerky. I gag at how low beneath me she is. I almost stop watching because she's proving to be a waste of my time and head back to the facility to let Jameson know his joke was hilarious because there is no way he could be serious with this chick. I am literally so amused by how disgusted I am with her that I am laughing, belly laughing in my car with myself until I catch a blank face staring directly at me from the corner of my eyes. I immediately stop laughing and return her stare.

*Ah, ha so this is why we like her. She's a bit bold.*

She doesn't falter, she's staring at me like she recognizes me and she should; considering I am in the facility often, but this is not a friendly, "Hey, girl, is that you?" stare, this is menacing, she almost looks scary until I smile at her. She breaks the stare at that point and speed walks back to her car and pulls out of there just a little faster than when she pulled in. I think it's funny, the irony of smiles. Something meant to be so warm and inviting could really mean the opposite depending on the variables. Barbara's got one of those smiles; I've practiced myself. It's a craft, really, a true art. You have to be able to put on, in any atmosphere, so I practiced in a dimly lit room and in the middle of a sunny day, I practiced with people and I practiced with my mirror. I practiced and practiced until it was perfect and my cheek bones ached. The thing about it was my smile seemed to flicker like a candle caught up in a breath. When I was practicing, I stared at my reflection and at first glance, it had a welcoming glow that promised comfort. Yet, as the seconds ticked by, an unsettling transformation took hold. The warmth melted to an icy gleam, and my mouth's curve seemed to contort into something a bit more sinister. It was as though the very air around my smile had grown teeth, ready to sink into my prey. I imagined her thoughts when I smiled at her. I bet she was caught between comfort and impending dread. I hope her heart raced and she could feel her pulse beating in her ears and finally that feeling of dread won sending her to race off to her car. I raise my eyebrows in boredom.

*There goes my canvassing for the night.*

When I get back to my place I can't get Sad Sarah. That's my pet name for her because everything about her is sad, from her oily hair to her scrawny calves. I just can't get her out of my head. Something is telling me I should pay more attention to her. I poke my lips out as I roll over onto my stomach and kick my feet about like a teenage girl on the phone with her crush.

I thought I could write her a letter about Jameson and I and she'd be so crushed she'd just leave, but that stare tells me she's a fighter so it would have to be something a bit more grand and more finite. This is love we are talking about and it deserves nothing shy of a grand gesture. I could show her the love we make, but then she could try to use that against me. No, that won't work. My brain trips up thinking about the two of them making love. I'm instantly nauseous imagining his hands guiding her hips like they did mine. I can't imagine her looking beautiful after climax with her deep wrinkles and charcoal gray circles. I realize I sound like I am being hard on her looks and that maybe I am jealous of her natural beauty. I can assure you I am not, I have a lot of admiration and respect for women who keep themselves up and don't look like they're struggling to get through the morning every day. It's just sad… Sarah could be so much more; you'd think after seeing me and feeling the energy from Jameson and I that if she wanted to stand a chance she'd step it up but no. She looks like bullshit, gray matter it's disrespectful to me and a man like him. I have a big day ahead of me tomorrow. I cannot wait to put this misunderstanding behind us and move on.

Walking into the facility today I feel renewed. I can't wait to be done with my volunteering. It is no longer serving me and work is growing more demanding. Today I don't make small talk at the nurses' station. I am here for one thing and one thing only; *him.* I'm sitting in the wide room with the small windows on each side in my chair as my group begins to shuffle in, amongst them is the love of my life. I don't make eye contact with him, in fact I am looking past him, but I catch a glimpse as he makes a Beeline toward me. I shift in my seat because today I am engulfed in confidence. I have Barbara's words etched in my mind and I am dressed to kill. He makes his approach and I look up to meet his eyes. I am wearing a very thin smile as I wait for him to say whatever it is he needs to say. *He hurt me and I am going to make him work for it.*

"Em, hi. Can we talk after the group? I am… concerned." *As you should be.*

"Certainly, Jameson, I am looking forward to what you'll be

sharing in group today, now would you please excuse me, we have to get started." The confusion on his face is laughable. Priceless even I wish I could have recorded this so I could show him later when we are at home together and we could laugh about it. I make sure to greet everyone brightly. I touch a shoulder, a hand, give a high five or a brief hug. I touch everyone but him. All of this done purposefully. He has to feel what it's like to crave me again. He needs to sit here and long for my touch and my attention, he needs to wonder what he did wrong and submerge himself in the discomfort like I had to do when he was so cruel to me.

Everyone is especially eager to share today, which means everyone's going off on a tangent and I am sitting here with a painted-on smile wanting to poke my eyes out. I am so bored beyond belief I am yawning in my head during each and every one of these shares. I need it to hurry up and conclude I don't have the patience for this. I am screaming inside with excitement. I just know he's going to want to rip my clothes off and take me right here as an apology for the bullshit he pulled before. I close my eyes thankfully, finally it's his turn to share so I climb out of my thoughts and tune in to him. *I'd much rather be climbing onto him.* A small laugh escapes me and I clear my throat and apologize to Jameson and ask him to proceed. I look to the woman on my left and raise my eyebrows and wink, as if to say, "Uh oh," she smiles. I hadn't seen her smile before, and her bags under her eyes they're practically gone and for a split second I felt happy for her,

I felt like saying, "Wow, look at you." I don't say anything at all, but part of me wanted to. Really wanted to.

Jameson interrupts my melancholy with his thunderous voice, "Thank you, today I want to share with you my thoughts and fears on navigating life outside of the safety of these walls. Right now we are thriving. We are also in a controlled environment, but outside of these walls there are stressors, temptations, and pressures; not all of them we can conquer on our own and I want us to have the courage to acknowledge when we are losing ourselves and seek help, know that no one will judge you for this, no one will think you're a failure."

Jameson's eyes meet mine in the midst of his speech. I think to myself there he is again that keynote speaker I first laid eyes on. The message has changed drastically, the delivery is also quite different, but the charisma is still there and so is the warmth.

"Know that there are people that love you and you should lean into that love because love, as we know it, is a force that transcends. It has the power to heal wounds both internal and external, and bring joy to even the darkest corners of our lives. However, love comes in many forms; it is not always a symphony of shared affection; that is romantic. It could come as a friendship." Here he goes again locking eyes with me, the timing of which is poor. "A parental bond, siblings, a doctor." I roll my eyes.

*Enough of this, he's playing with you.*

I have no idea what other bullshit Jameson spewed. I chose to tune him out. Finally, the boring silver rimmed clock with a white face and black hands reaches the hour mark so I can conclude this shit. "Thank you, Jameson, that was lovely and we appreciate you being open and vulnerable. But we are out of time for today. I look forward to hearing about everyone's future success. It has been my honor to join you in this journey to freedom. It has meant so much to me that you allowed me to include you all in my continued journey. I wish you all nothing but the best until we meet again."

*You can really put it on, can't you?*

The scrape of the shifting metal folding chairs makes me twitch. I'm still sitting, waving and hugging the last of the poor unfortunate souls goodbye when Jameson approaches me as everyone trickles out of the room and says, "Did you hear what I said, I am here for you, Em. I am not sure what you thought was going on, but I am here for you."

I click my tongue and sigh as I stare up at him. It seems I have lost him to her; to the gray. I simply sigh again and reply, "I heard you, love is not finite and through love we can heal." He seems rather pleased with himself at peace even. He leans in to give me a hug, I breathe him in and for a split second find myself standing at the crossroads before Jameson pulls away, the feeling of him letting go and it made me panic. I blurt in a rushed whisper, "If we weren't together, my Jameson, how do I know about the birthmark on your sack or the freckle on the tip of your dick?" Jameson pulls away so quickly and begins to chokes on his own saliva. Him being off guard sets my mind at ease. I feel like I am back in control so I taunt him, "Oh sweetie, what's the matter?"

"Em, you are unwell. I've never been with you! I'm going to have to alert the staff. I don't think you should be leading the group. Have you been taking your meds?" "You've never been with me? The videos of us in my phone say otherwise, oh and the ones of you and that bitch wouldn't look so good for her if they were to ever be seen, and don't call me Em." I calmly gathered my things and walked out the door, the metal clanging behind me. I left my id badge at the front desk. I wouldn't need it anymore after tonight. I scowled at the back of the night nurse who was leaning over the nurses' station, talking to one of the other nurses. She turned him against me with her poison and pussy I suspect. She may have won the battle but not the war.

My walk back to the facility that night was a peculiar journey. I had a culmination of emotions and the annoying moral compass in my head kept trying to explain that loving someone who doesn't reciprocate isn't uncommon and wasn't cause for the plan that I had brewing in my mind. But that moral compass doesn't understand what it feels like to be stuck in a dance where I'm the only one moving. Being stuck in a love where so much beauty lies in the purity of my emotions, in the sincerity of my affection that just isn't acknowledged, how is that fair? How is that something I should just take in stride especially after all we've been through. This pathetic excuse for Jameson standing before me is selfish, he's selfish for not letting my Jameson out and for not trying harder, for not fighting harder. For not fighting harder to love me!

I take my fingers to my temples to calm myself. He is lucky enough to have me, I am willing to fight for him. Plus, I got all the reassurance I needed. I saw him today, the real Jameson in the depths of his cool watered down green eyes, I saw the fire begging to be saved.

# CHAPTER 14

# HER ORIGAMI-LEIGH

I think I actually slept. They say sleep is the cousin of death, I wonder what that means for me? Do you get to relive things right before you die like I have been? Riding a vivid carousel of memories that gets faster and faster and won't let you off? Is that how I know death is upon me? I had no idea the depths of my mind's vault; that my mind was able to stretch how it did. I didn't think there was any room left in there, not for me. Not right now. I never dream anymore, not since she's consumed my thoughts, never. I guess my being awake in small doses was already filling enough nonetheless dreaming for myself.

But right now, my mind is purging. It was full of dreams and memories. At least I think they're memories. I am not sure of anything. Some of them I can say for certain happened, there's a certain physical response I can channel like being pregnant. I can feel the flutters in my stomach even now. Other details are foggy, like Jameson, but for most of them I can firmly admit that I didn't necessarily want to relive any of it, I could've gone without meeting Jennifer, I could've gone without losing Jameson in that way, and losing the babies though I wish I could remember their faces or the names we had planned for them… that's something I long for. I could find some solace in what I picked up about myself.There's an overarching theme in the story that is my life, something that made me proud. Love, I am consumed with love every inch of my being is rooted in love. The thoughts in my brain are deep seeded in love; they're just continuously folding like origami. One intricate layer after another. I just hope when this is over something beautiful emerges and not just the remnants of some crumbled paper or person. Because to be honest, there's been so many layers I don't know who or what will emerge in the end.

As I lay here in the depths of my subconscious, I can't help but want to stay. It's nice to exist. I can finally hear myself without hearing her. One would think me weak for just giving in to her and falling prey to the wants and desires of someone else, but I fought really hard, I did. I fought because of Jay, there was a little of me in that life I did everything I could in building a genuine one. I didn't care about how we got there. Once we were there, I tried to look past the madness and only remember the good. Most of that was me, the good, nitty gritty, the thick of Jay and I was all me. I had gone through hell to keep her away without tipping her off. She'd pop in every now and then and keep things interesting, but that scared me and fear is a weakness of which she latched onto and slowly but surely she swallowed me whole. I watched on in grave sadness as she ruined me and there was nothing I could do about it.

*Isn't that cute? Doesn't everyone reflect after they've done something fueled by emotion rather than thought? You could've done more.*

I frown and blink her voice away. I realize that I'm at a crossroad and no one will feel sorry for me if I am caught. They'll call me crazy, a psychotic bitch and they'll only be partially incorrect. They'll say I deserve whatever's coming to me and maybe part of me does, but not the rest. My heart aches because I didn't do enough to protect him from her. Soon, he'll know everything and I won't be there to shield his heart or cushion him as he falls. I tried my best to play against her and create some level of paranoia, but she's too keen too strong. I fear I may have made things worse for myself. I picture my ring with our initials carved in it "E&J" wondering how I could allow her to jeopardize what I worked so hard for.

This notion of allowing things to happen to me, to my mother, to my father grew into a monstrous ideal. It grew into an obsession that I could no longer control. I don't even know if I ever controlled it. My actions have had me questioning my own sanity. I began to agree with them, my mother and the doctors. She didn't and because of her I'll lose the one thing that has ever mattered to me, love.

True love, not her demented ideals of love but the love Jay and I share. We haven't seen much of each other lately. He doesn't know I'm still here. I see him, I hear him searching for me with pain in his eyes and his voice and I'm screaming out to him, but he can't hear me over her. The problem is the different lenses that we see him through. In one lens Jay is an immaculate representation of the prototype that is my love and therefore I love him because he is him. In another Jay is the prototype, there is no comparison and there never was.

My wedding day to Jay was literal perfection, intimate and picturesque in Napa Valley. It seems Jay had picked up that I had been drinking more wine lately and less whiskey. This was one of the minimal days I was truly present for, I fought so hard for this day. I didn't let the shame from unthinkable deeds get inside and scramble me up. I did not let insecurities push a new agenda. Since we eloped it was just us and dinner with our parents afterward so there was absolutely no sign of Barbara and no chance of her crashing. We did it at sunset. In a lace long-sleeved gown paired with a small underskirt, chiffon draped dreamily, mimicking gentle waves. My choice of shoe was a kitten heel adorned with a delicate pearl accent. A sunflower, its petals vibrant against my natural hair, was braided into my unaltered locks, which I had allowed to grow out without touching up my roots. I felt the warmth from the setting sun on my scalp and knew that my hair was glistening like it did that night in New York. I didn't wear my signature red lip on this day. I wore a neutral pink, a bronze blush and mascara. That was all.

My mother helped me get ready and I had asked her to close her eyes after she took a step back when I turned around to give her the full picture. When I said, "Okay, open," she silently gasped. I saw her chin begin to quiver as she tilted her to the side and brought both hands to her mouth to cover it. "Oh honey bee, you're gorgeous!" She let a tear drop, but this was a different kind of tear than the ones I had seen her cry so many times before. Looking in my mom's eyes at this moment made my throat raw. I was so harsh on her, so critical. Why couldn't I see then what strength it took to admit you didn't have enough love to give and to seek help for it when I read that journal.

Why didn't I give her credit for continuously showing up for me when she couldn't show up for herself? I expected more from her than she had to give and I never realized what seeing and feeling that must've been doing to her. I'm staring at my mom who I look just like in this moment, and she's beautiful, and my god she's strong. A rush of vivid memories comes crashing down on me as I hug her. Memories of my dad going to therapy with her, memories of us singing in the kitchen, memories of her holding me to ground me as I battered her and myself with my tantrums. I am sobbing into my mom's shoulder feeling overwhelmed and I can't get out any other words but, "I am sorry." She says, "I know," and I say again, "You don't understand, I am sorry." Again she says, "I know." I want to tell her, tell her everything about Jennifer, but she just says, "Bee, I know. Now let's get you married." The last I know will haunt me, and I curse that because anything that haunts me gives her power.

I wish I could go back there; to that day and stay there. I'd like to live in that memory because I was sure of myself unlike now. Now I don't know what to think of myself. What does all of this make me? I weep for my parents. I don't know the true depth of the hurt I have caused them. I weep for the children I want, but I fear for them. I don't know if I would love our children because they are both mine and Jays, or because I hand-picked Jay because of *him*.

What does this make me? What is at the root of it all. What lies inside? Is this obsession, or love? If it is love, can love be rooted in obsession? Is obsession not just being so consumed with someone, or something that you want to surround your being with the essence of them? Is that not just a component of love or admiration? Why must obsession be so negatively connotated? I don't get it. You see, I need to know for my sake when I'm forced back down that at the very root it was good, when it started it was good. I need to know that right now all I know is that I love hard and to a fault.I love my dad and I admired Jennifer. I loved my dad so much that I feared losing him like my mother had. It's just that one outweighed the other. Who can fault me for that! I honor Jennifer every day. I pay homage to her in my success in my confidence in my new sense of self. I became a better version of me because of her. Doesn't that count for something good? I am a complex person, a labyrinth of uncertainty in most cases except for love. I loved Jennifer not in a traditional sense but still. I loved her.

Love for me is all-encompassing, maybe it is slightly obsessive, a force that propels me into a realm where the boundaries between right and wrong blur into an indistinct haze. Some would say I have an irrational commitment that defies logic. I would say to be loved by me is chaotic where reason and order give way to the beautiful madness of unbridled emotions. The beauty of it surpasses all. To be loved by me is a thing of beauty. Like origami.

Jameson would fold origami cranes at the facility he sat for hours before he opened up and actually spoke; after folding these cranes he then strung them and they hung in the corner of his room. The cranes are a symbol of hope and peace according to Japanese folklore. He was searching for peace within and these little works of art took patience much like the patience required to begin anew. Or to be someone you've never been. His eyes were tortured, I recognized it.Like knows like. Maybe that's why I latched on to him so hard.

Before it took over, I truly saw him from a lens other than my own desires. He was folding each crane with care and precision, getting it just right, mastering control. He'd stare at his little creation when he was done and a small faint smile crept across his face. I think that was hope. After a while, I forgot what hope was. I forgot what it felt like especially after the wedding. After the wedding I didn't stay long enough to ever have hope again…

I'd like to think that somewhere in his mind Jameson knew it started from a place of admiration that grew into love. I never meant for it to end the way it did, she's got a way about weaving her words into your psyche that you don't believe there's any other way but hers. Jay doesn't know this yet, that my love knows no limits. My mother doesn't really know what I've done in her honor though she might suspect and Jennifer didn't understand that I loved her in my own way as well. I was Jennifer personified at times you could even say. My love for my father knows no bounds and I'm at odds with this, now remembering my wedding day. I had slighted visions of my mother never being there and it only being my father showing me love, I admit my recollection was skewed. There is no telling what else I may have gotten wrong along the years; either way I love that man with all that I am. I am selfless in my love. I feel like no one truly loves the way we should anymore. I don't know what's wrong with the rest of the world. What I do know is that I've got it right. Maybe it may be the only thing I've gotten right and that's according to my own bias.

*Let's ask Jennifer. Her opinion on your methods of love.*

In the beginning there was love, unrequited love, but I can hear the papers folding and the crisp slice when you slide your nail across the edge to solidify the fold. I can hear the folds in my brain becoming more and more intricate as the layers get thicker and thicker. And still I allow it; the layers to pile on so now I no longer recognize where I began and I no longer know what I am supposed to be. Origami is tricky, that way if you make the folds to crisp if you reinforce them just so, and you try to start anew, you will still see the folds that existed before, it will be hard to fold over them, you may accidentally refold the same line you tried to make a new one. You might as well throw the sheet away and start fresh, careful not to make the same incorrect fold again. Origami.

I've been fighting the fading of consciousness because It's easier for me to stay here in this daydream fully myself than to expose myself to her again in order to figure out what happened last night with Leigh, Barbara, and I. But at the end of the day what has always compelled me was love, so for Jay I will pull it together. I will make sure Barbara doesn't come back to haunt us.

# CHAPTER 15

# GIRLS NIGHT

My neighbor, as clueless as ever, agrees to girls' night. I was a bit manipulative in my request and I almost feel bad about it. She doesn't deserve to be used, and if she ever caught wind of my plans and realized I was counting on using her as an alibi, it would likely push her over the edge.

She has just recently acknowledged that she may need some help. Her mental health is declining. She hinted at depression the last time we spoke so when I invited her tonight, I used it as ammunition like the pure asshole I am. I said something along the lines of, she could use this night before she checks into a clinic. Come, let loose a little, have some wine, we will laugh, hell we will even dance and we will send you off to the repair shop in good spirits.

She laughed at my little repair shop joke and slowly accepted my invitation. Thank God. She mentioned that she wouldn't stay long or drink much because her husband had agreed to return with the children. They planned to check her into the facility together as a family. She didn't want him thinking she wasn't taking this seriously, or she wasn't committed because she decided to tie one on with me. She made it very clear she wouldn't do anything to jeopardize the fresh start they desperately needed. What she failed to realize is that I was in the same exact boat as her. We just had different methods for saving our families. Mine required a bit more flare for dramatics than hers, but she didn't have the thorn of a Barbara to deal with either.

I think what Leigh is doing is brave, but I can't say that I don't feel sorry for her. I know exactly how it will go when she gets in there. They'll drug her up, diagnose her with some bullshit, and claim she has some sort of past demons haunting her or childhood trauma that the shit stems from. Once they diagnose her she'll be a walking stereotype and anything she does, even if it is a basic human mistake like taking the trash out on the wrong day of the week, or maybe she cries a little too hard one night and sobs for a little too long, that's it; she'll be labeled manic or someone will claim she's having an episode; she won't be able to breathe without a stigma attached.

I think what she's experiencing is a bit more than depression based on my extensive hands-on field research, but nothing a little vitamin C, yoga, exercise and manifesting can't help.

Leigh claims she's having issues with her memories, that things are dredging up and she's afraid she's losing herself because she can't tell if they're actual memories or delusions. She says it's scaring her and it has been for a while because it's getting harder for her to just be her. By the time she realizes this, she doesn't know how much time has passed or what has transpired.

I've heard her story before I know it all too well. I feel bad for thinking so curtly of my sweet unassuming friend, but my God if she gets institutionalized and medicated she'll be even more of a personality-less zombie, but hey to each their own. I could never do that to myself again. Well, I mean I could if I truly had an issue or if it meant saving my family, but only if I've exhausted all other avenues. My guiding light to never being institutionalized again is that I can't imagine Barbara ever succumbing to such a feat, and nor shall I. As for my reasoning aside from Barbara, the gray of hospitals just does something to me now. I wouldn't subject myself to that again. Unless it was life or death.

In order to get Barbara to come I had to play to Barbara's ego because that is the only way to get her attention. We had been at odds and I knew she wouldn't go for the let's hang out without some groveling on my part. So I put on my best grovel and I apologized for my poor performance at work and my outburst regarding Jay. I said I just needed a vacation change of scenery and I was PMS'ing and that I literally was a weak bitch for a minute, but I've snapped myself out of it and I really just need a night with my personal boss bitch muse. She laughed and said she was worried I was wilting on her and turning into some desperate housewife. Eventually, she reluctantly agreed, but I think what truly won her over was the opportunity to look me in my face and dare me to say anything about what I witnessed her do with my husband. That was too good of a deal for her to pass up on. This type of situation is what her ego thrived on and I was serving it to her on a silver platter.

I was crushing up a charcuterie board of pills, a little antipsychotic, a little antidepressant, a little oxy with conviction churning a fine powder mix of what I'd like to call, "Get the fuck out of my life for good." I had smooth jazz playing in the background as I swayed back and forth. I felt as light as a feather. I wasn't the least bit nervous. If anything, I was anxious to get on with it. I could just taste my freedom. I don't know why I still had these prescriptions and filled them. I befriended the little old lady at the local pharmacy while in my scrubs decked out with all my facility badges one day. Jameson had scripts in his file for his impending discharge. I took them and filled them, paid out of pocket and she'd refill them every ninety days for me like clockwork. Sometimes they came in handy, other times I just tossed them. I don't know why I kept filling it, probably an ode to him which when I think about it is very odd and absolutely not a normal thing to do. But normal isn't really my area of expertise.

But I digress.

I was pulverizing these pills to a fine powder perfection because I was going to slowly poison Barbara to her death, an accidental overdose. I would run out to her car and plant some pills in the glovebox so that it made it seem like she had these with her and had already taken some prior to coming to my house. I would slide some loose ones in her purse for good measure as well. The only thing I couldn't set up was planting them in her home, the bitch had never invited me to her place. For all I knew she lived at the office.

My plan was to have Leigh arrive first to help me make drinks and food so she could be my witness as to not seeing me tamper with anything. I would never leave Leigh's sight. We would prepare everything side by side. It was beautifully and meticulously planned. I would finally be free of this leeching bitch after tonight.

Leigh arrived on time aka early just as I knew she would. We embraced when I opened the door and ushered her in; it was a stiff barely there embrace but one nonetheless. As we pulled away, she gave me this solemn look, different from the pitifully dull lost look she bore on most of the days I saw her recently. I have better memories of her smiling, being present. Leigh reminded me of my mother being the ever sound, reasonable and smart woman she was. Leigh was all of that and more a woman that I've grown to know and love.

Leigh deserved to be so much more than what she was presenting as she's one of those souls that you've felt like you've known forever even if you've just met, at least that's how she was for me. She was smart, but not in a showoff scholarly way. She was just in tune with things, I can't describe how she'd look at me knowingly when a wild thought was in my head or how when I was overly dramatic she was encouraging my calm. She was never a real overly assertive presence, but certainly she was felt more than this. But as I stare at Leigh, I am unsure if she was ever more than what I see before me right now. I clear my throat. "I was just about to start prepping some snacks and make a playlist, you remember my friend Barbara, she will be joining us." Leigh blinks a little too long and says, "Of course I know her, she's an extension of you unfortunately." I spat out my wine because Leigh was not the one to make snarky remarks like that, maybe there's hope for her yet.

We chatted laxidaisly about ourselves and she'd make comments about how she misses me and how she will miss me when she's gone. It is almost heartbreaking the softness of her voice, the words laced with tender emotion as if she's saying goodbye for good. I don't understand the seriousness here. We are friends I believe in spite of my initial suspicions of her, but we aren't that close for this night to be such a tragedy. And I plan to support her even if I don't agree with the method. I won't be visiting her in that hell hole, but I will absolutely call and plan a glorious welcome home for her.

I even plan to offer to help with the kids. I can be a good friend to her, too. I just have to rid myself of this looming soul sucking presence first. I don't want this to be a tragic night. I mean part of this night will be tragic for one of us, but it won't be Leigh or I.

The chimes from my doorbell play and I stand. The instrumental song playing on our doorbell is "Daisy Bell." I hum it as I walk down the hall toward the front door.

"Daisy, Daisy,

Give me your answer, do.

I'm half crazy,

All for the love of you."

I loved that song. I make sure to straighten my skirt and fix my hair and check the mirror by the entry for any lipstick on my teeth before I open the doors to let my frenemy in.

"Em," Barbara says brightly which throws me off my center a bit. "What's she playing at?" I say to myself. She winks as she breezes past me and I can't stop the heat that's rising in my body, or the raw feeling in my throat when I swallow. Barbara barely acknowledges Leigh and pounces on the whiskey and grapes I have spread out. "So, it's nice to see you making an attempt to take control of your situation" The way Barbara entered my space, my realm, and so coolly breezed passed me it hit me like a ton of bricks. It's so obvious I don't know why I didn't see it before. Barbara reminded me so much of Jennifer. Jennifer had been intrusive in my life, meddling in my relationship with my father and disrespecting my mother. However, the intent is the key difference between the two. I'm not sure Jennifer meant any real harm. She just wanted money and a life of leisure. She would've played nice if I let her, I truly think so. Barbara, on the other hand, is Jennifer except Barbara will bulldoze me in the process of taking everything from me that matters. The nurse just had the misfortune of falling for the same man as I did. She too tried to take something that belonged to me, that's never the right move. I giggle and shake my head fluttering my eyelashes. Life can be so poetic.

Barbara cleared her throat and I coughed because of the sheer audacity she had to interrupt my thoughts. I don't know why I was surprised, I shouldn't have been. I knew exactly what I was dealing with. I created her and her false sense of prowess over me and all. I revert back to Barbara's little remark and offer a response, "As a matter of fact I am. I can't stay home lying about waiting for the tide to change."

Barbara just raises her eyebrows and half a cheek bone as if to say she wasn't impressed with my response and abruptly changes the subject.

"And where is Jay on this fine evening"? says Barbara.

"Oh you don't know? With him being so high up on your list, I thought... your client list I mean," and I bite my bottom lip and smile.

Barbara raises one eyebrow and smiles back and coolly states, "If I knew you'd know."

Leigh shifts in her seat and reaches for a cheddar cheese cube, pops it in her mouth and sips her wine peering out at us from over the rim of her glass. You could tell she was extremely uncomfortable with the exchange. I knew she was fragile and I couldn't have her leave so I softly smiled at Leigh to ease her anxious look. "I have the best idea, let's take it back to college days and play, never have I ever!" I state with the boldest, brightest smile. Leigh remarks she's never actually played that game. Barbara says she is in and I cannot wait to let the games begin.

I usher us all into my study. It's my safe space and I need that comfort and a source to pull strength from, I also need a reason to leave said safe space to refill a certain someone's drink. I didn't want it to come to this, honestly. I know it will bring some sort of heat on Jay and I since she will be found after leaving our house. I am mentally preparing for that. I wish Barbara hadn't tried to insert herself into every aspect of my life. While we haven't always seen eye to eye, I forgave most of those times. However, she crossed the line when she went after Jay. That was an unforgivable offense. Jay was all I had.

*Never have I ever... murdered someone. Whoops      ::Puts finger down and drinks::*

# PT. 2

# OUT OF THE SHADOWS

# CHAPTER 16

# AWAKE

Have you ever had a repetitive dream? One that you can wake up from and fall back asleep just for it to pick back up where it left off? Or woken up gone through an entire day without thinking about your dream once just to go to sleep and have the same haunting dream start over from the beginning, giving you no reprieve from the parts of the nightmare you've already experienced? That's what life is for me now. It's like I've gone back in time and I am getting a front row seat to all the shit I've done leading up to this.

Part of me wants to acknowledge it all, the same part of me that relates to my mom that would rather accept it and deal with who I am than to pretend to be something I am not. I wish I could start over and be that genuine and loving and enough for the right people. Enough for my mom to love. Enough for myself. That part of me wants to relive it all and right my wrongs, but I know that's impossible. I could right them by admission. I could repent and I have repented, I think. Admitting them would mean ending my life. I don't know if I can willingly do that no matter how hard the morality strings are pulled.

Another part of me is oblivious and omitting all responsibility. There is no way I am responsible for what others forced me to do and therefore none of it is my responsibility. There's also a small part of me that would do it all again because whatever I did was necessary. I don't know which part of me I resonate with more, the lines are blurred.I'd like to wake up, I'd like to stop the recurring dreams and I'd like to put an end to it. But I can't, not yet. I know this. It has nothing to do with the wine. I remember now as I begin to drift. I remember.

****

My eyes begin to flutter and revelations of this dimly lit gray room creep into my line of sight. I am hesitating because I am not sure of what is to come when I truly open my eyes. I've been visited by the ghost of Em's past all fucking day and I am not really up for more visitors. I am lost in my own train of thought when the nauseatingly sterile scent of antiseptic assaults my senses and it does so slowly as if marching in from a distance and growing closer and closer. That damn beeping sound comes back getting louder with every second that passes.

A tingling sensation in my toes causes me to wiggle them and a numbness in my ass makes me squeeze the muscles, which hurts as if I'd broken my tailbone. I roll my neck and it sounds like bubble wrap. It's the most awful sound I may have ever heard. I attempt to sit up and am immediately stopped and strangled back down by a plethora of wires and chords, the beeping speed has increased and I blink more times than I can count and take a few deep breaths and finally stop to take inventory.

*You're awake.*

Usually, I am much more collected than this, but panic begins to set in as I am realizing where I am. I don't recall how I got here, or why I was in a hospital bed. I'm feeling uneasy and I am not sure why. I'm also feeling immense disappointment and that doesn't really make sense.The hangover I thought I was experiencing was a dream? Was this all a dream? Why the memories? Why the history lesson? Why make me relive Jameson?

I feel the tears welling up in my eyes and they sting as they trickle down my cheeks. My eyes do a blurry water-logged scan of the room and I am not alone. My mom is asleep in a chair in the corner of the room. I can see my dad's coat lying over the edge of another chair but no sign of him.

I'm fucking freezing; the blanket that's covering me is paper thin and my fingers are poking out from under the blanket where it seems I have been tucked in. I want to move, but my body has no strength. I try to tune into my body harder maybe with each attempt at movement I can figure out why the fuck I am here.

*You remember...*

The beeping monitor is beginning to slow its pace, I realize this monitor is attached to me. I want to unplug it, but I know a more ludicrous alarm of noise would just follow suit. I need a mirror, I need to see myself, I need to look myself in the eye. The table on the right of my bed is full of flowers and the table on the left holds 2 teddy bears and some cards and pictures. One of the cards seems to be drawn by a child. The realization slaps me hard and I remember Leigh and her children. That card must be from them. But Where is Leigh, has she come to see me? Does she know why I am here?

My mother begins to stir in her chair and I have it in my right mind to wake her and plead with her for some water. My mouth is so dry I have no saliva to drink. But waking her means I would have to deal with her. I am not ready yet.

There's shuffling right at the entrance to my door, the aroma of hot coffee punches me in the face. The door flies open and my dad walks in and kicks the door closed. "Hey, hun, here's your coffee. If you want to go home and get some proper rest and nutrition, I am more than happy to stay here. I will call you if she happens to wake up on my shift." I have my eyes slanted so finely that no one would be able to tell my eyes were open. My mom must have woken due to the intense roast my dad brought in. She thanked him sweetly with a kiss on the cheek and he grabbed the air of the cheek kiss and placed it over his heart. What a croon he could be.

My mom rolled her eyes and smiled as she adjusted the recliner for the leather chair; she was just sound asleep on; so that she was now sitting up and took the steaming coffee cup from my dad's hands.

"I still can't believe it came to this. I can't believe we are here and she is laying there in God knows what condition." she said before she asked my dad if he had seen my doctor on the way in. My dad said doc was due in 30 minutes and then he would begin rounds and they probably had a solid hour and a half before he'd make it to my room. Dad paused, leaning on the ledge of the windowsill, and said, "How about this: we walk to the deli a block away and get some food in you. It will be good for you to get out of this room, you've barely left her side since the accident."

*Accident! Was I in a wreck? Oh my GOD am I paralyzed. Accident? Is Jay okay?*

Before I could continue worrying, my mom countered rather hastily, "Stop calling it that, it wasn't an accident. You've been downplaying this for far too long. She tried to commit suicide! Our daughter tried to kill herself because of us. We are to blame.

We didn't love her enough to do what needed to be done for her. Instead, we wanted her to love us and not hate us so we let her carry on with her delusions and look where that got us, almost childless and God knows what she will be when she finally awakens."

My mom is now sobbing uncontrollably into my dad's chest. I watch barely breathing as I don't want to draw any attention to myself. My dad embraces her completely and places multiple kisses to the top of her head and says, "Let's get you out of here. You need some air and some nourishment and you're right, hon. I never wanted to accept the signs even when I witnessed them first hand like that day at the office. I knew deep down I was just too afraid to admit it." *That day at the office?*

I am impatiently waiting for my parents to get the fuck out of my room so I can't sit up and piece some things together. I don't know why they are talking about suicide unless Jay is trying to help cover upmy tracks? Would he do that for me? Did I actually go through with it?

*Remember! Deep down you remember!*

A voice in my head is screaming at me, and I am beginning to panic. The beeping on that fucking monitor begins to speed up blowing my facade of still not having come to. My mom practically sprints to my side to grab my hand. I am willing my eyes to stay shut, but it's as if someone is forcibly peeling them open. I hear my dad yelling for a nurse and my vision begins to blur and anxiety sinks in because I don't want to answer to them right now. I don't want to answer to anyone because I don't have the fucking answers. I can feel my body begin to sweat as the ringing in my ears intensifies and then black just pitch blackness and silence.

# CHAPTER 17

# DEAR JOURNAL

Once again, I'm in the gray. Maybe I should embrace the gray instead of continuing to fight against it, it seems to want me here more than anyone or anything else. By no fault of my own I always seem to end up back here, maybe this is my true destiny. Here, inside these walls. If I let her have her way it would be, I am only here to bide my time. I guess it's safe enough here. It'll be my turn soon. I know they want this. My mom's probably crying tears of sadness to hide her tears of joy. She's probably singing, "I told ya so," in her head. She's always wanted me in here because she needed me to be a sad soul like herself. She didn't want to do this journey alone so she wanted me roped in with her.

My dad is keeping it cool. I know him. I can do no wrong in his eyes. He knows this is a mistake, but he's probably pacifying everyone, especially her. I'll do this again. I have no choice, but this time I'm doing it for what's outside of these walls not what's inside. I am doing it for them; Jay, Aaron, and Alivia. I'll play along to be the damaged soul they all want me to be and agree with whatever the therapist says. I will work quickly and efficiently. I will even ingest the poison for a spell, but they don't know her like I do. Barbara is a snake—she sheds her skin and begins anew. I wanted to cry when I found out I wasn't successful. I put it all on the line that night to get rid of her and now she knows it was me. She hasn't said it, but she knows and she'll use it against me one day. I can't say I am not uncomfortable with that knowledge. One would even say I was a little afraid of what she may do for revenge. It's my turn now, time to give the people what they want.

All eyes are on me, I can hear the faint whirring of a circular fan. I can't feel the air it's producing though I wish I could. I stand up, fix my shirt and I smile politely to the group and clear my throat, "Hi everyone, my name is EmaLeigh Barbara Jameson. My husband calls me "B" short for Babe. My parents call me honey bee, and my little loves call me mommy."

I sweep my overgrown feathered bangs out of my face. I haven't dyed it since I've been out of commission so my dark brown tresses are now auburn and on full display. "I have two beautiful children, Aaron and Alivia, and I'm voluntarily checking in for treatment of my depression, Dissociative Personality Disorder and the symptoms I suffer from associated with my schizophrenia. It was really hard for me to acknowledge those terms. It is something I have never done before. These illnesses have caused me to pull away from my family so much so that I attempted to take my own life while caught in a manic delusional state.

"I am now on my meds and am here to get coping mechanisms and get stronger to be the best mother, daughter, and wife I can be... I know this road won't be easy and I may fall, but I will get back up and keep going. Thank you." Once I finish regurgitating the absolute bullshit I've been spoon fed before, I glance up at my family because they're here to support me on intake day. My parents, my husband and my babies.

I'm only here because I tried to kill Barbara. They think I tried to kill myself, minor misconception on their part. Hard to explain without implicating myself in an attempted murder case. So I once again have to bit the bullet and do time in the gray.

I drugged Barbara and got her drunk on whiskey; Jameson, to be specific because that's her favorite and I hid seven pills in her pours within a four-hour time span.

It was touch and go for a minute there, but she pulled through apparently seeing as to how I am here being checked in for attempted suicide as opposed to being hauled off to prison for murder.

According to the police report my children were in California with Jay's parents for fall break. My husband was away on business and that checked out. The report said that he had all his itineraries and proof of when meetings attended. Everything was noted, where they were held and what he did in between. No surprise there, he's always been meticulous.

Upon Jay's arrival home, he found me in my study sprawled out on the couch, cold to the touch and stiff. I spent 72 hours in a coma after my stomach was pumped. Toxicology reports were… well, I should have died.

I asked my family about Barbara. I did it in a way that questioned if anyone had let her know about my condition. I told them I didn't want to leave her hanging at the office. My family replied rather matter-of-factly that there is no other Barbara, just me; I don't have the capacity to process the bullshit so I play along with them.

My family says I have no neighbor with children, that my odd loyal sweet friend Leigh doesn't exist; my husband says my neighbors' children are mine. Sick. All of them, the children are innocent, though. They look like Jay with hints of *him*. Which makes my heart scream.

That first group was the only time my family was allowed to join. I had to do the rest of this bullshit on my own. This time there was no color to look forward to and there was no Rob. I know I am a married woman and I am not saying I would have cheated on Jay, but I am not opposed to flirting if I needed something badly enough. Jay visited 3 times a week. The children came on Saturdays, My parents on Sundays. Each visit was more of the same. "We are so proud of you, we will get through this, just give yourself time." The only ones I truly enjoyed were the children who brought out a different side of me. I couldn't wait to be reunited with them full time. I can't believe they even exist. I do question how I could have no true memories of raising them. It makes not only my mind, but my heart hurt. I feel my heart more when they're around like something more pure is reaching out to them from the depths of me.

I have spent ninety days in the gray so far and I've accepted I am a little bit crazy. If I wasn't crazy when I got here then I certainly am now. I take the pills when my gag reflex gives me away and other days when I can manage it, I hide them until I can spit them out.

I wrestle with a lot, but what I have come to accept is that Barbara and I are one in the same. She visits me with her ominous glare and her teasing words calling me weak and letting me know just how much I've let myself go. I'm better at ignoring her now, but I'll never tell my family that she is still around, though. They'll say I'm unfit for release, they'll say I'm a danger to myself and others. Barbara and I seem to have an understanding these days. I tell her how much of a cunt she is for making me block out my children. She tells me I never should've had them. I then tell her to fuck off and she does until something or the other peaks her interests again.

My therapist says I have intense advanced Dissociative Personality Disorder. That mine is so warped that I truly have out of body experiences. He explained it like so, "EmaLeigh when you are Barbara, Em and Leigh do not know that Barbara is also EmaLeigh, the only one of you who knows it all is EmaLeigh. There are triggers and traumas that we are working through that cause you to allow EmaLeigh to be stifled and Em or Barbara to take over. You truly do not know when you are Leigh and you believe you witness Leigh interacting with her children that that is actually you and Leigh is just an extension of you."

How fucking ludicrous does that sound. He needs to be in this chair, not me. But I'm due to go home tomorrow so I've got to play this right. I hate when I have to take the meds. I can't think straight. I don't recognize myself in the mirror. I can't have a decent conversation until they wear off. My first order of business will be getting placebos.

The day has finally come; Jay is here with the children to take me home and I'm bursting with excitement to get my life back. I want to kiss my husband and have him make love to me. I want to play with my kids. I just want to be. I see my little family walking through the doors and my gaze locks on each one of them. Aaron has Jay's eyes, Alivia has *his.* They nearly knock me over when they run up to me and grab hold as I'm saying goodbye to my therapist with my little koala bears clinging tightly to my side. From the corner of my eye a sweep of short dark hair hands my husband a box and a folder. My skin is boiling as I watch her hand graze the top of his. They exchange a few words and my antennas are now up. My first thought is to lunge toward her. But I see Leigh outside of the locked doors through the small picture framed window shaking her head no and giving me a very corny thumbs-up. So nice of her to be here to support my release from the gray. I make myself a mental note to not mention of it to my husband or parents.

Aaron tugs my arm. "Mom, you okay?" I look down at my boy and smile in awe. I almost forgot they were holding me and I snap out of it and tell him I'm fine. My heart swells, I must be a decent mom, they don't seem afraid of me, they don't regard me like a stranger though I feel they are. The car ride home feels new to me. It's familiar but foreign at the same time. Like I am seeing all of this from a new lens. At home, there are so many pictures of me and them and their birthdays and my head hurts a bit because why weren't these pictures up before? Or were they? I scan the room frantically for my favorite image and relax a little once I see its frame peeking out from behind a Christmas photo of Aaron and Alivia with Santa. A bit of sadness washes over me that I don't remember these things. There's this nagging voice that says I never wanted a husband and kids to begin with and I bat it away.

My parents are visiting today despite my husband warning it may be too much for me, but my mom insisted and promised she wouldn't stay long. She hugged me so tightly and whispered in my ear she was so proud of me after asking me if I filled my scripts before coming home. At that I rolled my eyes.

My dad says I can take as much time as I need so that when I am ready, I can hit the ground running and my office will be waiting for me at Ingenuity Recovery whenever I want to return. My eyes must convey my confusion, but my dad ignores it. He simply taps my thigh knowingly. A quick Web search later that evening tells me pops is the owner and CEO. Was this public knowledge? Fucking Barbara, no wonder I could never go to the board meetings she didn't want me to know I had the upper hand my father being the fucking owner. This bitch. I can't react right now because everything's too fresh. I have to bide my time, and I will. Loving mother, picture-perfect daughter, doting wife—I'll play the role they expect of me on the road to acceptance and recovery. And then, I'll find her and finish what I started.

It's been six months, six months of going to outpatient therapy sessions and six months of swapping my pills for sugar pills. I'm a great fucking mother and no one suspects a thing. Leigh and I have wine nights from time to time. She tries to tell me to be careful; she doesn't live next door anymore and that makes me sad, I miss her. She's also seeing a therapist, but she's really taking her meds because she says her family is everything to her, she can't lose them. While Leigh and I may share in some similar struggles we handle things far different. That's the issue between my friend and I. She can't lose her family and I won't lose mine. This is where Leigh loses me every time.

I have had some pretty non eventful weeks which is good for a person in my situation. I need life to be as lowkey and normal as possible. That's why when tonight took a turn I wasn't prepared. I had been doing everything right. I was in my study and had just shut my laptop down from another session of scouring the web for Barbara, when Jay walks in, fuming tears stream down his face. I couldn't even react to his condition when he throws a box at me and slams a folder on my desk complete with his wedding ring.

Now this has my attention. "Babe, what the fuck?" I say after him. I start to get up, but I figure I better look into what's got him in a tizzy. I opened the box to find a lock of fiery red hair and a photo of two young men and their parents. *His* face scratched out and Jay's circled. I open the folder, and inside are my commitment papers from the first time I was committed to a psychiatric hospital. And another torn sheet of hand written paper from a binded book. I remember now. The first time I was stuck in the gray and the fire got me through. These papers are from the time we met. I smile at the memory. The screech of tires rudely snaps me out of the warm memory and I race down the steps. I call out for the kids and Jay and get no response. Gone.

I pick up the single torn sheet and read.

****

Dear Journal,

Doc says writing is therapeutic and I should do it daily. So, I'll start today with a letter to my love. Dear Jameson, love doesn't come easy, it requires hard work, dedication and most of all passion. I know we had what it took, but you were too distracted to see it for yourself. And really, how would I know that you'd never truly leave me for her? I needed to be certain. You couldn't give me that certainty so I made it so. I'll honor our love though, my fiery Jameson James. Outside of these gray walls, Jay is waiting for me and through him I will love you eternally. Today I'd had enough. I'd warned you, my love. Our once promising love story lingered as a poignant memory, now drowned in the silent tears of heartache. I am being poetic for you, babe. I will do that from here on out. In honor of us.

You see, Journal, when I confronted Jameson he told me that I was imagining things, that we weren't together. He told me he was due to go home soon and I needed to mind my fucking business when it came to him and the night nurse ,also known as

Sarah, so I don't ruin it for him. That's when I knew that dark haired bitch bewitched him like B had done my father, side swiping my mother.

When I first got here Jameson, the ungrateful bastard, spent a lot of time strapped up hunched in his chair. Sarah wasn't there! I was there! Brushing his hair, feeding him, sneaking him treats, I'd kiss his lips and suck his dick and he told me he loved me, too. Maybe not in words but in his eyes, but it wasn't love once they'd watered him down with that poison and he was "sane" enough he started fucking the nurse. I should've killed her like she deserved, but you see, that would've required way too much planning and my resources were limited. But him, that'd be easy enough. I'm a generous person and I thought if I gave him one last chance to stay, he'd see the light... but he rejected me. When I snuck into his room that night to plead our case to get him to see clearly, he was so overworked and anxious and he pushed me away so coldly with such disgust for me, it rattled me to my core. He was getting ready to call for someone so I injected him with a paralytic. I stabbed him with the syringe directly in his neck as he was stomping toward the door. Rob had set me up with an endless supply of the good stuff. I kept some here and some at home just in case. The world is a crazy place, you never know what you may need. It's comical and kind of sad what men will do after a little sexual innuendo.

Once Jameson couldn't move, I emptied a bottle into his mouth and forced them down. I straddled him as I watched the fire go out of his eyes and his dick grow limp. I am not cruel. I wanted love to be the last thing he saw, but in the corner of my eye was a photo of two young men and their parents. That's when I first saw Jay and I knew it was destiny.

In conclusion, my dearest Jameson, I had visions of you and I when we first met here in the gray. Where you breathed life into me and yet I was forced to love without you, but there's beauty in this madness now. I can love you through him.

When I finish reading the journal entry, my jaw drops and my body instantly breaks out in hives. There's only one reasonable explanation for this bullshit and it's Barbara. I am not sure how Barbara managed this shit. When did she piece together who Jameson was? Is this why she's been getting so close to Jay so when she dropped this bomb he'd go running to her!?

I didn't kill him. I did not kill Jameson. I loved him. That nurse is the only one who is responsible for his death. She killed him with her dark hair and seductive body, she did it! She had to have...

I open my phone in an attempt to call Jay, trembling in a storm of emotions. My tremors cause me to open my photo library instead of the green phone symbol I was aiming for.

The clip of Jay cheating on me with Barbara begins to play.

This is the last thing on earth I want to watch right now, yet I can't look away just like I couldn't that night. The eyes in the video that meet mine are horrifically familiar, the auburn hair that's swaying around the frame draped over Jay... my eyes cross and I see my reflection in the glass of my phone, my reflection in the video. I see... me. My pulse filled with uncertainty quickened as I grappled with the consequences of my, her, our actions and stared at the evidence that had at least two different handwritings knowing one of them did not belong to me. I couldn't stop the chill that crept up my spine trying to decipher whose handwriting it was and why. I had weaved my way in and out of situations my entire life, always the victor, always with a plan. As I sit here holding the end of my life as I know it, it's eerily silent.

# CHAPTER 18

# WITHOUT THEM

There's a heavy knock on my door, the heavy hollow knock you'd expect from the morning shift nurse waking you up. A stark contrast from the warmth of my husband's body cuddling me and kissing me awake. Or the laughter from my children drifting down the hall like the sweetest alarm clock. No matter where I look it's white. I can't really say if it's better than the gray. I think I would've preferred the gray. But I don't have any choice in the matter now, I lost that right some time ago. I've been waking up from the same nightmare for four long years. My son Aaron is almost a teenager and my little girl Alivia is almost done with baby dolls. I can't believe that stage has come and gone so soon. I've missed it all. Quite literally I missed it all, even then.

These days I wake up as EmaLeigh and it's been easier as time went on to stay EmaLeigh. Only this recurring nightmare reintroduces me to Em, Barbara, and Leigh over and over again.

A nightmare I've been trying my hardest to defeat, but have learned that no amount of therapy can erase the demons. I don't hate those three, each and every one of them shaped me into who I am now. I am proud of the woman I am now. I have overcome some daunting things. Just because I don't hate them doesn't mean I wish to ever share my life with them again. I don't think there was a time all those years ago I was ever EmaLeigh. Except for my wedding day. They had far too much of my time. Time I cannot get back; they took up far too much of me. My wedding day was one of the best days of my life; that day is the only memory I have that really truly belongs to me. It stands out so beautifully in a sea of darkness it's the only light. Everything else was like I was being puppeted.

I find myself reflecting back and journaling a lot grappling with the complexities of my existence, the fragments of a shattered identity slowly piecing themselves back together. Living with split personality, schizophrenia and clinical depression is like being trapped in a labyrinth of mirrors, where every reflection is a different facet of myself, each vying for control. When I relive those days whether in therapy, memories or nightmares I still struggle to discern how I could be buried so far beneath Barbara and Em; and I mourn for Leigh how she tried so hard to alert me to things to get me to wake up or to at least persuade Em in the right direction; all of her efforts in vain.

I've acknowledged the biggest hindrance I had in gaining control of my illness was my denial. The constant battle for dominance, the relentless tug-of-war between even just Barbara and Em was exhausting. The scariest part was how rare my moments of clarity were. In those fleeting moments, when I was just EmaLeigh, I was able to breathe just to be suffocated once more. It's not like that anymore. I know that those women inside me will always be there, but I am managing them now.

Of course, I live with the fear that at any moment, the facade will crumble, and I will once again be buried within. There are days when the darkness feels overwhelming, when the weight of my own existence threatens to crush me. I long for the day when I can look in the mirror and not want to recoil at my natural hair color and see myself as beautiful without a domineering lipstick shade. I still have attachments to the qualities that made me feel like something. One day I'll sever those attachments, but for now I am keeping them in check. That's the only way I'll see them again.

There was nothing left here for Jay once he handed me that box in my study, so he left. He packed up the kids, put the house on the market and left. Left me here. My family is on the west coast now, Jay needed stability for the kids and he leaned on his parents to help out now that he was a single father. He didn't cut my parents out of the picture. The children spend spring break and a week in the summer with my parents and they have an open-door policy. Though my dad's not one for the west coast so they haven't been out there yet. I couldn't thank Jay enough for not writing them off along with me. I don't actually know if Jay has moved on, he hasn't mentioned it neither have the kids, but I don't know that they would even if he had. They call once a week and send letters and pictures to keep me up to date with all the happenings in their lives. Initially, even though he facilitated the contact for the children and I, Jay didn't say a word to me for the first two years. These were two very long draining years for me and I needed him, I longed for him, me EmaLeigh, the woman he married, the woman he knew before she took over fully. I know that I loved him. I know deep down Jay knows that too even if I couldn't beat out the one that loved Jameson. I wish Jay would have talked to me so I could've at least explained, if he could just look into my clear eyes now he'd listen if not to believe me. I know that at the very least I could give us both closure, but he wouldn't then…

The third-year things turned a little in my favor because Jay spoke to me without it having to be about the kids. He began to be cordial; he'd ask how I was getting along and if I had identified my triggers. He'd inquire about my meds and dosing. And now as of late he's been almost friendly. He asked about my plans for release and how active of a mother I planned to be. He expressed his concerns and rightfully so and that nowhere in the foreseeable future would I see them unsupervised. I understood all of that and agreed wholeheartedly to whatever he and the kids would be comfortable with, only today when we spoke, he finally acknowledged my apologies. I have been apologizing to him daily for years. He never so much as told me to shut up; he simply did not acknowledge I had even existed. I was apologizing to Jay for lying and for refusing the help I needed and for not telling him that I knew Jameson before we met. I was not nor would I ever apologize or take responsibility for Jameson's death. Even as Barbara, Em loved Jameson so much she wouldn't have let anyone hurt him.

I saw the journal entry and I don't care what it says I did. I didn't kill him, Jennifer yes, Em took care of her and I have to live with the guilt of a crime that weighs on my heart but not my mind for the rest of my life, but Jameson no. Jameson's life isn't on my conscience. One day I would find a way to clear my name. I'd comb over everything with a fine-tooth comb and prove it to him and maybe then I may have a slim chance of getting my family back. Fickle hope has sparked in me because he threw me a bone; after all this time he finally said he forgave me!

Aaron had just finished telling me about his baseball game and how he hit a double and brought the guy on 3rd home while making it all the way home himself; by stealing bases. I could hear how lit up he was telling me about it. I was beaming on the other end of the line too, when Alivia was done telling me about her dance class and the tap number she was doing to the song hit the road jack I heard Jay say, "Let me speak to mommy, Liv." My heart about screamed because this was the first time in a long time there was no venom in his voice in reference to me.

When Jay got on the phone, my heart rate began to sprint. He told me exactly how hard it was for him to accept that I would be in his life for the rest of it; due to the children we created. It was a stab to the chest. He went on and told me it took a lot of prayer and therapy to get him to this point, but he revisited everything he could recount from our years together and from the reports he is privy too from my therapist. He was swayed by the severity of my illness and he was mad at himself. He couldn't believe that he had missed so many red flags he even battered himself about choosing to ignore them because he loved me. He read my therapy notes and said his jaw dropped at the sheer amount of distorted and fragmented memories I had shared. He said some of the things I shared never even happened.

Jay was speaking to me with hesitation in his voice like each word he had to muster up the courage to say, like it pained him. I knew what it was, he felt like forgiving me was betraying his brother. It was laced in his tone. My heart ached for him. He said that realizing how in depth my illness is and how truly sick I was at the time caused him to struggle with his feelings toward me for a long while. I was not only someone he once loved, the reference of our love in the past tense stung because I still very much loved him. But I was also the mother of his children. In the end, he said he couldn't imagine what it must've felt like to be trapped in a prison of my own mind within a personality that was so evil and opposite of the true you. He continued a bit winded now as his pace began to quicken like he just had to get it all out because if he didn't, he wouldn't be able to ever attempt this again. Jay told me that his heart had been too heavy carrying the weight of the hatred he had for what my sickness turned me into, but forgiveness was the first step towards healing for both of us.

I sighed the biggest sigh of relief and gratitude and I thanked him repeatedly and offered my excitement for a chance at normalcy with him and the children and that's when he stopped my heart from beating and said he welcomes co-parenting in the safest most effective way for the children, if a relationship with me is what they want, but he is seeing someone. And even if he wasn't, there is no level of forgiveness or maturity that he could ever reach that would allow him to forget that I murdered his only brother in cold blood, and that venom that had disappeared from his voice just a few minutes ago was back with vengeance.

I shook my head and sobbed into the receiver. I tried to tell him I didn't murder Jameson. This is not the first time I tried to tell him, my attorney, my therapist, hell the fly on the wall, but it always went in one ear and out the other. Just written off as the ramblings of a crazy woman. So of course, this time on the phone with Jay was no different and I knew it wouldn't be so my plea came out as a soft whisper because a very small part of me questioned it, too. There was no way I could be one hundred percent sure, but it wouldn't have made any difference, no one had believed me, not even my father. In everyone's eyes I was a murderous psychopath with a history of manic episodes and a very strongly worded journal entry that proved my admission to the crime. It wasn't my handwriting in that journal entry. But according to psychologists those who suffer from Dissociative Personality Disorder can even speak different languages with a near perfect accent so handwriting changes were not uncommon. That was all anyone needed to hear to write off any of my credibility for good.

But I've been clear minded and proactive in my treatment for almost two years now. The first three were a bit rough at times and I am able to recall the things I've done through Barbara with much more clarity and acceptance. I admit when I was living as Barbara, I was obsessed with Jameson and as Barbara I did love him. I loved him in a very scary way, but I did not kill him. I won't say that the thought never crossed Barbara's mind, but I know that we didn't kill him because what I failed to share with everyone, as it was a mute point, was that he was already dead when we went in to put Barbara's plan in motion.

Barbara's plan was to allow the night nurse to catch her and Jameson in action. She was going to use the paralytic so he couldn't stop the rape she intended for him, but she was never going to kill him at least that wasn't the plan for the night he passed away.

I know that I am not completely innocent, I did stalk and rape Jameson. I was also the one responsible for Jennifer's death, but Jennifer's death is not what cost me my family. Jameson's death did and his was a death that I had nothing to do with, might I add. Revealing my part in Jennifer's death would put the nail in the coffin to me ever seeing my family again and I cannot allow that. I'll let God deal with me when I get to the pearly gates cause I will be damned if I admit that shit now when I am so close.

Next year I am eligible for release as I was convicted of involuntary manslaughter in connection to Jameson's murder, but offered the insanity plea due to their lack of physical evidence aside from the journal entry and I was sentenced to five years in psychiatric prison. I had the ability for parole and to be released to a halfway like house that required me to attend outpatient therapy after 18 months. I was denied parole at 18 months because I was still exhibiting concerning behaviors. Behaviors that I was not responsible for, but with my track record I didn't have a leg to stand on and I couldn't explain the occurrences myself. It's now year four and I am finally at a place of contentment where I have hope for the future but hope is fickle.

Jennifer's death is still unsolved and I fear everyday it may come back to bite me in the ass. My moral compass points north, but I am so close to seeing my kids again and there's a sliver of selfishness in me that I let live and I've decided to let sleeping dogs lie where they may. No one accused or suspected me even after the news of Jameson broke, except my mother.

On a day that my parents came to visit and announced they were engaged. Go figure.Just showed up on a normal visit and dropped the bomb; there was no foreshadowing in phone conversations, nothing. I almost wasn't happy about the news, but the flush to my mother's cheeks and the healthy weight she was carrying, let me know she was healthy, happy and medicated.

I made the poor choice of mentioning Jennifer in congratulating them, something along the lines of, "Well, at least one good thing came out of the loss of B." I saw the color drain from my father's face and my mother faint gasp. I had to tell Em and Barbara to simmer down at the very mention of B. I apologized immediately, my father whispering, "I know where it came from, hon, it's alright." My mother painfully whispered, "It is okay, honey bee." Then an octave softer, "I know," and cupped my cheeks in her hands and let a tear drop. She patted my thigh as I stared at her blankly, not sure exactly how to respond other than dropping my head down.

My father was talking to my therapist so he was preoccupied. All I knew was that my mother was going to keep this secret with me. She conveyed that much in the way she looked in my eyes when she said she knew. I would forever be indebted to her, or maybe this was her way of thanking me. I mean, without Em intervening in the manner in which she did, my mother wouldn't be getting ready to marry my father right now. Or maybe she wanted to make amends for the weary bits of my childhood. Whatever it was I was grateful and I will never mention Jennifer's name again out loud for the rest of my natural life.

# CHAPTER 19

# RESENTMENT

Resentment isn't a strong enough word for the feeling that echoes the halls of my soul. I've spent many nights drumming my fingers on the desk, on the counter, on the mattress impatiently waiting for the Universe, God, Karma, something to hit her. Something to sweep in and take everything away from her like she has from me. What's left of them are the framed photographs that sit across from me in the rooms I inhabit — a snapshot of happier times, a relic of stolen moments when they were here when they existed, before her. What's left of me is merely a shell of a person, a cold, calculated machine just running on autopilot barely a will to live other than *her*. My chest remains tight, my breathing always swallowed. I often catch myself staring at my reflection, tracing the contours, searching for what was stolen from me. She has altered my very being. I hate her, all of her, for brazenly taking something that could never be returned. Don't you think someone should pay a consequence for this sort of offense? I do. In the absence of tangible evidence, I am choosing to be the judge, jury, and executioner. I've already convicted her. There's no doubt in my mind she's responsible. She admitted it all: only the ramblings of the disturbed aren't concrete enough for me to seek justice through the system. The only thing I can't figure out is why me? What did I do to deserve her wrath?

I've let so much time pass. There's a testament to be said about my level of patience. I've had an overwhelming yearning to confront the thief for years now. To demand an explanation for the theft of my source of happiness, my immense sadness, the darkness that now consumed me was her fault and I needed to know why she did it. It's not that I didn't have the courage, I did. It's the feeling that confrontation wasn't enough. What would confronting her really do? I would feel no vengeance in that, there would be no suffering on her part and that's all she deserved. It would be my personal mission to ensure it. I rehearsed the lines, a million times exactly what I would say to her when I had the chance. I went over the cadence, my tone, my facial expressions I even thought of what I'd wear, maybe something that would strike a chord in her. Yet, when faced with the opportunity to speak, my voice faltered, imprisoned by the echoes of revenge knowing I wouldn't be satisfied with the result and I would have blown my cover.

The passing days seemed like eternities, but I steeled myself ready to unveil my wounded spirit and unleash my fury on her already decrepit world. She is far brighter than what she is given credit for and she is far more disturbed than she is perceived to be. None of that matters to me. Am I to believe it was mere chance that led her to my world to shatter my heart not once but twice? No one is that lucky. There's something bigger behind this, maybe it is my life's mission to end her evil existence. I realize doing so would not make me any better than her, but at least beneath my newly acquired veneer of ruthlessness lies a conscience that struggles with the actions I am willing to commit in the name of redemption. I know there's not a single remorseful bone in her worthless body. I can see the emptiness almost daily when I look at her.

The problem with being a psychopath is that you don't recognize when you've encountered another. She wouldn't recognize me if I stood in front of her and kissed her. She doesn't have a clue I've been watching her. That the roles have since reversed.She doesn't know that the only things that matter to her in the world now are also what matter most to me, and I will take them from her and dangle them in her face just out of reach. There's a small piece of my heart that rejoices in this, knowing I have access to what she wants most of all and that I will also ensure she never has again. The problem with always watching and studying other people is that you're too consumed with them to notice that you're being watched yourself.

Leading up to my big move I had spent most of my free time setting up her downfall, I tried my best to delay or prevent her release for as long as possible so I could get things in place. It worked for 3 years. She is up for release in 2 years, but during that time I made her the most unstable individual. I made sure she didn't get the right dosage of meds, I left menacing voicemails to Jay on her behalf, I even harassed her mother via letters and texts. I showed her doctors concerning journal entries and drawings that I claimed to have found amongst her things. She was none the wiser, when confronted with the evidence she had no recollection. She even believed she had done these things. How could she know any better locked away behind these walls where she belonged? But I couldn't do that forever. I had to begin work on what mattered most. This next phase would be tricky. It would be a fine line to cross. Some may think it odd or disgusting, but with enough trauma bonding and my involvement with the children I could very well pull this off. I already had an in, which gave me a slight advantage if I played my cards right.

EmaLeigh is preparing hard for her release. It is all she can talk about. She just cannot wait to get to them. I still have eyes and ears in her facility so I get updates. Her release is the only thing she has left to look forward to. The release I am going to spoil.

It wasn't long after I moved that I had lunch with his mom. She loved me and was ecstatic that I was so close. She told me how everyone had been getting on after the ordeal. And that everyone benefited from a bit of counseling, but otherwise they were thriving. This woman was a saint because she told me she had no ill will toward her, that she was so happy she was getting the help she needed. She hoped that in honor of Jameson she would turn this sickness around.

They obviously worried for the children. Having mental health disorders on both sides of their families was scary; so Jay was extremely vigilant and he was always in tune with the children. He stopped traveling for work and promoted one of his best guys allowing him to sit back as CEO/COO of his firm. I was disappointed to learn that everyone was still in touch with her parents. I personally didn't think they deserved access to the children, but I had no say in the matter yet.

It only took another month before Jay and I were getting together for lunches or hangouts with and without the kids, it was like old friends getting reacquainted. Winning over the kids was my main concern so I doted on them. I did all of the young motherly things with Liv, like hair and makeup and shopping and I was a safe space for all the school drama and boy talk. I went to Aaron's games and worked the concession stands for his parents' chaperoned field trips. I was an intricate part of the family dynamic. I was like a glorified fun aunt until I wasn't.

One weekend evening I was babysitting for Jay. He had a client dinner and his parents were out of the country on vacation. I kept at the opportunity plus, the kids were great, I truly did care for them. The night was typical me in leggings and a hoodie hair typed up in a sloppy bun; not an ounce of makeup just some chapstick. It was only ten at night and the kids were already in bed sleeping. I was spilled out over his couch three glasses of wine deep, watching the Titanic, when he came barreling through the garage door. He had a few drinks with his clients and was in a rather lively happy mood. He asked if I was up for a shot and to play some darts in the man cave. I told him I couldn't be more ready to whoop his ass. We were two shots and a game in when Jay grabbed me by my biceps and turned me to face him. He said he just wanted to thank me for jumping into the kids' lives like I did and now that I was in it, he can't see how we ever got along without me. He said he was battling his attraction to me because albeit a very long time ago I was once the object of his brother's affection. Though most of it was delusional, I was never really with Jameson. He was a lunatic, but he could fuck like it was nobody's business and I did care about the guy as friends so I saw to it to make sure he was getting the best care at the facility. If it made him feel better to claim me I could care less and I paid no mind to it. I was climaxing every night and he knew when he was of clear mind we weren't together even though he said he was going to change my mind and make me his. I had a lot of love for Jameson and he did not deserve what happened to him. But life isn't fair.

I told Jay that I too struggled with my growing attraction for him, but I reminded him I was never with his brother. Jay didn't need to know that Jameson was blowing my back out from time to time. I reiterated to Jay that I cared deeply for Jameson and I sympathized with his struggles, but I only ever truly had eyes for him. Jay tilted his head and furrowed his brow in a bout of shock and disbelief and then he pulled me in and kissed me hard. That night I let Jay take me on the pool table in his man cave while her children slept two stories above.

****

26 months later...

The alarm on my phone went off and I stretched, pointing my toes and yawning. I rolled over to the left and reached my arm across the bed to feel for him. My fingers jammed into his side and I rolled closer as his body was radiating a welcoming heat, I wanted to be closer, too. I stared at his face, the fine lines around his eyes and the salt and pepper locks spewed about his head. He is in his upper 40s now, but he's got the body of a 25yr old with rock hard abs, protruding pecs, and that delicious "V" that points down to his glorious manhood. He's seasoned and fine and not surprisingly mine, finally.

I wanted to start us both off on the right foot today because today would be a trying day for us all. So I slid the oversized T-shirt I wore to bed up over my head and placed it to the side. I slid my panties down to my ankles and toed them off. I traced my fingers along that delicious V and felt him flex his ass muscles in response to my touch. I began to trail kisses down the path to his manhood when I felt his hand caress the back of my head and sleepily ask what I was doing. I looked up at his sleepy minty green eyes and said, "Shh." He smiled and closed his eyes once more. I dipped under the comforter and wedged his boxers down inch by inch until his manhood sprang free. I put him in my mouth and pumped, needing to feel him release, needing to know that I did that for him. He moaned softly and I picked up my pace working him, milking him until he finally gave in to my prowess. He sat up and hooked both hands under my arms and dragged me up to him and kissed my forehead, nose and then lips.

"Don't worry," he said, "she's doing great. I have no concerns. I'm actually really proud of her. I talk to her doctor regularly and he also has no concerns. Babe, look at me," he urged. "She's going to love you." Aww my pure hearted guy thinks I'm concerned about that devil liking me. I could care less. I hate her down to the roots of her hair. I hate her. What I hate even more is that he is seeming to care about her again. I didn't know he was regularly communicating with her doctors like for what!? Jay and the kids were my family now and over my dead body would she walk back into their lives, she's the plague and I'm quarantining them. "Babe, I'm just concerned for the safety of the kids and really do they have the mental capacity to understand why they can't just go with Mommy and why Mommy is dangerous and why Mommy should never be alone with them?" I was going to continue on my tangent, but Jay stopped me and said, "She's their mother, babe. She'd hurt herself before she hurt them of this I am sure. They love her and they need the healthy her in their lives."

It took a lot for me not to cock my arm back and slap the stupid out of him. I was their mother figure now, they didn't need anything from that psychopath. I guess I'll have to show him better than I can tell him. Jay hopped out of bed completely naked and headed toward our bathroom. His ass was rock hard and the muscles in his back flexed with each stride, I was salivating. I quickly hopped out of bed and chased after him. He laughed as I grabbed his waist and playfully humped him from behind. He knew though I wasn't playing at all and I wanted him to give it to me. He spun around to me and kissed me deeply. I was melting with eagerness for his penetration, but he ended the kiss and didn't do much as touch my pussy and whispered, "Later, baby, we don't want to be late and keep her waiting. It may cause some unnecessary anxiety." If thoughts could kill, EmaLeigh would be dead exactly where she was standing.

We are meeting this woman for breakfast and heading to an arcade after where she thinks she will parade around like mother of the year until she sees me; until I whisper sweet nothing in her ear and send her spiraling. I will flash my left hand in her face and rub the kids heads and kiss their cheeks. I will press up against Jay all while smiling directly at her. She won't recognize me at first, but I can't wait till it clicks and when it does, she will snap and land herself right back where she belongs all on account of me pushing her to her brink.

We pull into Della's Deli at 10:37 a.m. and Jay is literally shaking. He's been honorary since we were running almost forty minutes behind on account of me. I staged a little morning sickness and made mention of how I may be late. I am not late, but I knew that would give me more grace than making us late for putting on makeup. I wanted EmaLeigh to sit there and wonder if we were coming whether she'd been stood up. I hope when we walk in she looks pale and her hands are clammy from anxiety. I hope she looks ghastly disgusting and the children cower away from her.

The kids hop out of the car anxious to get inside to see their mother, but before we knew it, she was headed outside toward our car, hair a chocolate brown with auburn highlights cut into layers with the longest one just beneath her bra strap. Her skin was dewy and a thick layer of mascara coated her long natural lashes and that was it, there was no other makeup and she was beaming not at all the sad sack of shit I was hoping to see. Jay hit a light jog and the kids sprinted practically tackling her to the concrete. They hugged all 4 of them in one big huddle completely forgetting I was there. A gut punch if I ever had one. Jay then cleared his throat and said, "EmaLeigh, I have someone I'd like you to meet." I stepped out from behind the truck and smiled wider than hips and extended my hand to hers and said, "Hi, there it's really so nice to meet you." Cupping my left hand over hers, making sure she saw my ring shining. What she did next told me everything I needed to know about Ms. EmaLeigh. She slid her hand from my touch and used her left hand to swipe her hair from the right side of her forehead to the left, clearly showing me the ring Jay gave her when they were married. Why was she still wearing that, regular fucking psycho?! Her eyes were scanning me, trying so hard to put a name to my face.

# CHAPTER 20

# RECONCILIATION - EmaLeigh

I am counting down the hours until I can finally see Jay, Aaron and Alivia again. Everything will be easier in person. I am so nervous I can't even imagine eating without my mouth watering to vomit. I get to see my family again this morning. It's surreal to say. We are going to an arcade after we meet up to get something to eat for breakfast. I have strict hours in my new recovery center and I don't want to be late for curfew so we made plans for an early day of fun. Missing curfew results in losing day pass privileges. I cannot allow that to happen. My one hope is that my children aren't afraid of me. I know Jay, he is too good of a man to tell them I am a murderer and that I am not worthy of their love or a second chance. He would have spared me and said Mommy is sick and she is getting the help she needs so she can get back to you guys for good. He would have given me the grace I don't deserve. Telling them I killed their uncle would have been a lie either way because I did not kill that man. I always thought he selfishly killed himself leaving me without so much as a goodbye. I hated Jameson for that. I've worked through those emotions now and my obsessive behaviors. One of my therapy goals is to refer to myself as one person and to stop dissociating myself from Barbara, Em and Leigh. When I disassociate I relinquish control I am no longer the captain of this ship. I acknowledge their wants as something intrinsic in me, but I can no longer be a morally gray excuse maker for my actions whether I recall partaking in them or not. I am still learning everyday, but I can honestly say there hasn't been a trigger strong enough that made me call on Barbara or Em. I am EmaLeigh through and through.

"EmaLeigh, let's go! It is morning session time!" I roll out of the stiff mattress at this facility and head to the sink to brush my teeth and pull myself together a bit. My bottom lip was chapped and I bit the hanging skin pulling too far causing my lip to bleed. I pressed my crimson-stained lips together hoping the pressure would calm the sting. My eyes met the mirror recognizing the all too familiar hue of my lips. I couldn't breathe for a moment my hands were shaky, I regurgitate bile. I raised my eyes to the mirror once more and a sinister smile took shape. I acknowledge the smile, the color red certainly left its mark on me, which reminds me I need to take my meds. "EmaLeigh, let's go, dear, the doc wants to get you in first so you can make it to your very important meeting." the nurse on staff says with a smile and she's right I need to move my ass. I finish primping, grab my ring and rush to the doc's office.

I've been sitting here for an hour and a half now, granted I arrived early but they are late, really late and it's worrying me. I don't have a new cell phone yet so I can't call Jay to see if everything is okay, but it should arrive today. I was just too anxious to see them to put it off till tomorrow, it will be at my residence when I get back and so will my parents. Who will ask me every single detail about today.

I see a truck pulling in as I'm pacing the entrance of the deli trying to talk myself off the cliff and a female in the passenger seat. It's been a while, but Alivia is not grown and so I can only conclude that Jay brought the nanny. At least this is what I'm going to tell myself until further notice. I won't let this minor inconvenience distract me. I'm running full speed toward my children and him. My feet can't move fast enough until we all finally tackle each other in a four-way huddle. I can't help myself from peeking through the cracks of our arms to lay my eyes on the mystery woman. She looks familiar, but I can't put my finger on it. She's blonde though with a bob ish haircut; that's not Jay's type, she couldn't possibly be with him. Could she?

Jay broke our huddle first, but before pulling away whispered in my ear, "You look really good, Em. I am so proud of you." That set my soul on fire. Just for him to extinguish it when he introduced me to the blonde woman as his fiancée. It took me less than ten seconds to know I didn't like her and only these few hours to realize she isn't who she says she is. She's after something, her intentions are not pure and I will protect my family at all costs; they've been through enough.

The day had gone as well as you could expect with the intruder invading my time. I did pull Jay to the side and tell him I would've appreciated a heads up. This day was supposed to be about us reconnecting not an introduction to your fling. He apologized and corrected me saying they were engaged and he thought it best to just rip the band-aid off. I rolled my eyes and sighed deciding I wasn't going to give this any more energy than it deserved. She wouldn't be around much longer. Jay nudged me and pulled me into a side hug before we went back to join our kids in ski ball. I made sure to lock eyes with what's her name and wink. And it hits me; what is her name? They never even made mention of it. She glared back at me. Check.

Back at my facility I paced the floors trying to tell myself this was okay and that I knew Jay and I weren't married any longer. I tried to put my hope in check and to accept reality. I knew I was a brat to the woman today. I couldn't help myself. I will be better next time, I will apologize... my thoughts trailed as I caught a glimpse of the blonde woman at the front desk. I'm not usually in the library recreation space at this hour, but I have never seen a blonde nurse or maintenance person or even front desk clerk here before. Not that shade of blonde with a bob. I start to take steps toward the nurses' station when the sweet janitorial staff woman stops me to ask if I was okay, "You look like you've just seen a ghost, darling, you alright? Take your meds this evening?" I shook my head. Yes, in this facility you should be independent in taking your meds. It is expected because of the progress you made at the last place and this is a transitional place back into society where it is your responsibility to put your mental health first and take your medicine and see your therapist regularly. I don't actually know, though. I don't remember if I took them this evening, I'm sure I did this morning. I probably did tonight too so I wouldn't mess up. Not with so much on the line. When I turned my attention back to the front desk she was gone, either my imagination was playing tricks on me, or Jay's fiancée was just here.

I obviously had to find out so I made my way to the entrance and approached the desk cheerfully. "Hey there." I said to the front desk guy on duty, casually. "Got a new member to the crew?" I asked, gesturing with my lips to the front door she obviously walked in and out of. "Oh Sarah? Na, she was just saying hey we go way back."

"Oh okay. Well, I was just doing some late-night reading. Going to head off to bed now."

"Uh huh, I bet you had a full day; hard to sleep after that, night, Em."

"Yes, it was, and it's EmaLeigh," I said slowly and with suspicion because I all of a sudden didn't like the tone he used or the fact that he called me "Em."

"Right, it's EmaLeigh now, got it." I walked away not glancing back because the vibe that man gave me tonight was creepy, but what the fuck was that and Sarah?! Sarah. I scrunch my eyebrows because Sarah… why does that name make the hair on my arms stand up?

# CHAPTER 21

# ACCORDING TO PLAN - SARAH

It's been three months and I've slowly been ruining "EmaLeigh" as she likes to call herself now. I've been running her mental health into the ground, she's turned into a typical schizophrenic, a paranoid ball of shit who can barely control her emotions. She's convinced someone is out to get her. Her paranoia is at an all-time high. She calls Jay crying at all hours of the day which is extremely annoying, but I play the role of sympathetic fiancée so well. She's literally building the case against herself for me, but what makes it even better, actually what makes it hilarious is because she's right. Someone or someones should I say are definitely out to get her and I won't rest until she's successful in her next suicide attempt. She still doesn't know who we are and if she does, she hasn't admitted it to herself because she's scared to death. She's like a mouse caught in a trap, if she says anything else too crazy, she'll look like the unstable psychopath she is and if she does anything it'll be even worse. She's made one attempt to call me out and it fell on deaf ears. She forgets I share a bed with Jay and pillow talk goes a long way. She told Jay she sees me at her residence building at night talking to the clerks and nurses and she thinks I am trying to keep her away for good. She told him I show up with dark hair and red lipstick just to taunt her. And I do.

I hear Jay now on the phone with the nut job begging her to calm down. I've lost interest in him. I haven't lost interest in the sex, good sex is hard to come by and I am too preoccupied to go out and find another. But outside of the bedroom he is a weak bastard. He's too emotionally connected to this woman's well-being even when he knows firsthand what she's capable of. I get she's the mother of his children, but I was here a fucking stellar step-mom willing to take on the heavy load of mothering for the sake of these kids. I care about them, but not enough to spare their mother and now I don't care enough to stay; now that what I want is taking shape so beautifully. Years in the making my plan finally in the depths of its clandestine prowl. She was once the maestro of malice and now I am orchestrating each chord in perfect time. I feel it creeping back into the corridors of my soul, the happiness that she stole. Each phone call brings me joy. I know he feels the same when I give him updates when we meet up in the hushed corridors of secrecy. Where only the secrets we share coil and twine. I feel as though I've been patient enough. It's time for the final act to commence, and the curtain to fall. It would be a beautiful night if she fell on the night of a blood-red moon, since she likes red so much.

Tonight, my brother has dyed his salt and pepper locks a fiery red clay and he is sporting a fresh pair of green contacts. Tonight, my brother will walk the halls of Em's place and haunt her. Tonight, my brother will inject her with a paralytic and whisper sweet nothing into her ear. She will think she had a nightmare until she sees him every waking minute of her day. He will go to the coffee shop she works at part time on Mondays, Wednesdays and Fridays. He will be at the playground during her 1-hour unsupervised playdates with her children. He will make the next week a living hell for her. Like she has for me, for us. I knew she was obsessed with Jameson, the whole place did. They just thought it was a crush, but I knew this bitch. I knew her well and I knew what she was capable of. Jameson was a genuine friend of mine, we only started fucking because I noticed her crush and I wanted her to find out. I wanted it to drive her mad. I cared for the James family. I did, but I had to sacrifice Jameson for the greater good. Jameson didn't deserve that, any of it, but she meant more to me than anyone else in this world.

I poisoned poor Jameson snuck in right before I knew she would get there. I did fuck him one last time, that's how I caught him off guard. Injected him with the paralytic and then followed it up with another syringe enough to kill a horse. I crept out of Jameson's room and finished her journal entry off for her admitting to killing him. The journal entry she didn't even knowingly write. I handed the box of evidence to Jay myself when she got released, and I waited patiently for her life to begin to unravel.

Jennifer was my sister. We were only a year apart. We were thick as thieves the closest and she took her from me. My brother was already in a bad place after his break up. He was staying with us and between jobs and Jennifer's death broke him. My brother, Max, went on a bender, lost what little bit he had left and ended up in rehab. She shattered my entire world. Left me here to pick up the pieces for both Max and I. Jennifer loved her father and she couldn't wait to marry him. She always felt Em was a bit odd, but she chalked it up to not being that much older than her and marrying her father; she assumed Em just needed time to adjust to the thought. She kept giving Em the benefit of the doubt even when she caught her following her a couple of times. Her biggest mistake was never telling anyone but me. She didn't tell that psychopath's father or mother, she just dealt with it and hoped it would stop the more they got to know each other. It stopped alright, after she killed my sister and left her to rot like she was nothing in the street. She treated her lifeless body worse than a dead animal. I will never forgive her. Even if Jesus Christ himself asked me to grant her forgiveness I would look him square in the eye and say fuck off before I forgave her.

To my detriment and heartbreak, I had no proof only what I knew that stayed in the silent chambers of my mind. I know Jennifer was with Em that night because she told me! I was on the phone with her when that murderous bitch got to the bar. My sister wouldn't lie about that. We told each other everything, she'd have no reason to lie. I told the police that, but it was my word against hers and since the bartender pegged my appearance as a possible person she was with I looked like I was just covering my own ass. I couldn't believe the incompetence of the police force. If they weren't going to pin down this bitch I would do it myself. When I told my brother everything, that was all the motivation he needed to get clean and sober. He knew I would need him and he wanted her to pay just as much as I did. We hold the knowledge of Em's sins, our hearts had to bear witness to her dark desires and carry it in my soul. Jennifer, we will not fail you.

# CHAPTER 22

# THE AWAKENING - EmaLeigh

I don't know what's going on. I've been taking my meds, but I feel manic. I feel like I am going insane. I am seeing things. I am seeing Jennifer. I am seeing Jameson and now I am not fully convinced I didn't kill him. The doc has changed my dosages, Jay has come to see me weekly this month as I haven't seen the kids. This was my choice. I don't feel like myself and I don't want to say or do anything that scares them. I don't want to lose them again. Jay is trying to be supportive and he is concerned rightfully so because we were having breakthroughs—the biggest being me having an hour alone with the kids each week which was ruined when I cause a scene screaming and pleading for help because a man was following us. A man that didn't fit the description of anyone in a 5 mile radius of the park on foot according to the police. Jay was empathetic, but paused the solo time for the time being. But he doesn't understand and I can't explain it. Now when

I look at him, I only see her. I can't get her face out of my mind. She's haunting me. Sarah. Why is she haunting me?

I can't sleep at night when I close my eyes. If it's not Sarah I see then it's him. I can practically feel Jameson standing over me staring. I opened my eyes once and saw him there. I screamed so loud and slammed them shut wishing him away, wishing to wake up. The nurse on staff at night came rushing into my studio apartment at the residence and gave me a sleeping aid and said night terrors are a common thing and that she would let doc know I was sufferingfrom them. She doesn't understand either; they aren't terrors, he's real, I can feel him, and I can feel them; Barbara and Em and a little bit of Leigh. They're trying to communicate with me, but it's so muffled under the meds I can't hear them. I need to hear them. I want to hear them. Maybe they can help me understand what's happening to me. I need help. I need their help. I can't sustain another night like this. "Em," I whispered into the silence, my voice barely audible over the din of my thoughts. "I need your help." I felt stupid and weak. But I couldn't stop myself from saying it again. I was willing to let her take over. I wanted to die and wake up as Em. There was a moment of stillness, as if the very air around me held its breath. Then, slowly I drifted to sleep.

"SARAH!" I sat up drenched in my own sweat panting. "Oh my fucking God, SARAH." I am gripping my sheets and my knuckles are turning white when I hear, "That's right, Em, Sarah…" coming from a male voice that I didn't recognize. I called out, "Hello, who's there?" With a confident stride, the man approached my bed side with a familiar face, dark hair and eyes. A small item clutched in his hand which he then slid across the bed, the sound of light wind rung through my ears as the plastic object met my comforter. It was an old keychain with three young children in the photo, it had seen better days. Two little girls and a little boy arms hooked over each other's shoulders; a tense silence filled the air. My intruder was moving about my small place. I don't know what he was doing. I was too busy studying the faces in the photo trying to connect the dots so I knew why he was here. I don't know why I didn't call for help immediately. I should have. Before I could register what was happening, the man who I now recognized as the desk clerk, had pinned me down and a sharp object was stabbed into my neck. I tried to scream but nothing came out. I tried to move but felt nothing. He was kneeling on my arms. I felt the pain of the stocky man, but I couldn't do anything about it. He just knelt there staring into my eyes smiling and then laughing. He knew he was hurting me and he was enjoying every second of it.

The smile, the laugh and then it hit me like a ton of bricks. This is the man I thought Jennifer was sleeping with, this is the aged version of the boy in the photo, this is Jennifer's brother, and Sarah is their sister. I was screaming inside. I just wanted to hug my children one last time. That's all I could think of. I had to fight my way out of this, but how? My eyes scanned the room as he relieved me of his body weight and I just lay there. He's planting evidence at my place. He's got vodka and open pill bottles on my bedside table and he's placed our latest family photo next to me on the bed. This man is going to kill me. Maybe I deserve it, maybe no matter how remorseful I am or how innocent I am in the case of Jameson, I deserve this. I close my eyes and inhale for as long as I possibly can, guessing life would be slipping away from me soon, as I don't know what he injected me with. I open my eyes trying to stretch them as far left as possible so that their faces are the last I see when a whiff of perfume floats by me.

I quickly move my eye right and there she is smiling dark haired and red lipped. She opens her mouth to speak, "I want hatred to be the last thing you see. I want you to die knowing that your kids will call me Mommy and that I am responsible for stealing your very existence from you as you did to me. I want you to burn in the fiery pits of hell knowing that Jay will be making me cum for as long as I will have him because he will be my husband, and I want you to know one more thing, Em. I killed Jameson James." I felt another stab and life as I knew it had ended.

# EPILOGUE

The soft hum of medical equipment filled my ears as my body began to stir, my eyelids fluttered open and the pain of the fluorescent lights beaming down made me wince. The all too familiar smell of bleach and antiseptic spray overwhelmed my nose. Through squinted eyes I could see the gray walls and my heart immediately sank. I must be stuck in my nightmare again. My entire adulthood had been one long prison sentence. Stuck in my own mind, stuck in psych wards, stuck in hospitals, always stuck. I don't know if this is reality or my subconscious, but I am scared to find out.

I open my eyes a little more allowing them to adjust to the lighting, but angling more toward the large picture window where I am greeted by a softer glow of dawn filtering through the curtains. For a moment, I just lay still, mostly disoriented and uncertain. The room was empty aside from a vase of sunflowers and a framed photo, the last photo I remember seeing before... *There we go, remember.* The memories flooded back with startling clarity.

I remembered the terror of that fateful night, the red tinted sky and them. The wheels in my brain were turning rapidly now and I was struggling to keep up. It was like the screeching of tires, a distracting unnecessary noise doing donuts when you just want to drive straight. I begin to stretch my body. I know I will be weak. I can tell by how stiff I am that I have been here for a while. There are no tell-tale signs that this is reality and not a warped version of my previous dreams, and that is what I am so desperately searching for.

I heard the creak of the hospital door and because my body feels like it's ninety-five years old, I can't turn fast enough to see who it is before I hear, "EmaLeigh," from a breathy warm voice, choked with emotion. "Last time I checked." I replied, Jay finally appeared in my line of sight as he reached out to grasp my hand in his. "You're awake." I nodded. "It appears I am, the great awakening." I tried to joke. A smile tugged at the corners of Jay's lips which made my heart flutter for just a second sending me down a rabbit hole of memories: the warmth of his hands pressed on my breasts, the feel of his lips on mine; until I abruptly dropped his hand remembering Sarah, his fiancée. Jay didn't seem to read into my abrupt gesture and asked if there was anything he could get me. I replied with, "Yea, an explanation for starters, why am I here?" He laughed softly and pulled up a chair. "Still feisty as ever.

Em, you tried to commit suicide again, you were manic and apparently not taking your meds, your parents think a controlled facility may be the best option for you going forward. You've been asleep if you will for just over a month." I was probably millimeters away from an eye bugging out of a socket with how hard I was rolling my eyes. I never once tried to commit suicide, even when I was responsible, I truly thought I was taking care of Barbara. But you can't explain away suicide with a murder plot doesn't exactly bode well for a gold star on your mental state.

I gasped as the wave of what I saw last consumed me.

"Where's Sarah?"

"Oh, uhm probably at the cafeteria with the kids. I'll text her to bring them up, you sure you want to see them now, you just came to? I should add, your parents are in California. They've just arrived this week they've been to visit frequently."

"Yes, now. I want to see the kids. Jay, have you introduced my parents to Sarah?"

"No, they've exchanged pleasantries over the phone, but I hadn't introduced them. Honestly, Em, this occurrence has strained a lot for Sarah and I and it wasn't at the forefront, but I suppose they will meet today since everyone is here."

"Mmmm, I suppose they will."

My babies trampled through the door and jumped on the bed

completely oblivious to the tubes hanging from me and the fact that I had just awakened. It hurt like hell, but I didn't mind it, not for them. For them I would endure anything. They sat for about an hour telling me stories and making me laugh until the nurses kicked them out, after the doctor had already come in to give me my run down. My eyes were glued to Sarah the entire time. She didn't utter a peep Jay probably thought so highly of her sitting there not taking any attention away from me, he had no clue he was sleeping with the devil.

I heard the rumble of my dad's voice in the hallway complaining to the nurses they would only stay a minute; they just needed to see me before the door swung open. Sarah, who was now blonde again tried to slide out behind my dad's entrance as Jay was collecting the children, but I stopped her. "Oh hey, Sarah, thank you." She tilted her head and nodded, not making eye contact with anyone and I winked as she walked out of my room. My dad paused a second furrowing his brows and pressing his lips together as if he thought he recognized her. I didn't give away the big reveal just yet, I knew for a fact she could feel the ice in my words as she was leaving. If she were smart, she'd skip town as soon as possible. I don't know what my fate will be after this episode, but I will find a way to get to her, she should take heed.

My dad kept his word and only stayed 5 minutes. Four minutes and thirty seconds of that was my mom draped over me sobbing, begging me to stop doing this to myself; telling me my life was worth it and that I had so much to live for. My dad was trying to shush her, but she ignored him altogether. She was right, I did have something to live for and that was love. Theirs, my kids, Jay's, and I'd have all of it. My dad had to use the jaws of life to pry my mother from me but he finally did. I apologized to them before they left. I was truly sorry for what I had done and what I will do. While I was happy to see them, I was grateful for the nurses rushing everyone out. I wasn't in the headspace to be overly pleasant; I had work to do.

Throughout the day, I went through all of the essential checks, consulted with the physical therapist to map out a regimen for regaining my strength, and engaged in a brief conversation with the on-call psychiatrist. I was acutely aware that every action I took would be scrutinized meticulously, so I aimed for perfection in all endeavors. So I could recover. The scars of my past would never heal with loose ends fluttering about. They would constantly reopen and be an ugly reminder and that just won't do. I shift a bit in the bed and take a deep breath in, the tray in front of me is full of bland food. A sturdy knock on my door is met with a, "Come in," and my nurse shuffles in with a white plastic bag and a note attached. "It's not New York but it will do- Jay." The aroma of shrimp fried rice smacks me as I open the white Styrofoam container. I smile and look up at the ceiling; all of a sudden I feel renewed, my sense of purpose restored, my determination far greater than it ever has been. I ate the Chinese food feverishly as if I had been starved. When I was done, I pushed the tray aside and I laid back in the stiff bed of the gray that embraced me, a place that took so much life from me, restoring it once again.

This time I am embracing the gray. The warmth of the setting sun peeking through my window caressing my skin as Jay soon would again. This was a promise of a new beginning, Sarah and what's his face should've stayed in the trenches loathing me from afar. But in their ill-fated attempt to take me out they did something far greater. Before I drifted off to sleep, I opened the small compact mirror my daughter carried with her today and told me to hold on to it for safekeeping, or in case I was too tired to get up and do my hair and makeup I could do it in bed. I laughed when she said that. Thinking about it now, a smile adorns my lips. I would sleep tonight actually sleep because I knew no matter what tomorrow held, *we* would face it together. I opened the bedazzled pink compact, met my own eyes in my reflection and whispered, "Well hello, B. I am awake, are you?"

www.ingramcontent.com/pod-product-compliance
Lightning Source LLC
Chambersburg PA
CBHW032008150726
47990CB00005B/1880